MODERN VIKING

A JOURNEY OF LIVING BY ANCIENT VALUES IN A CONTEMPORARY WORLD

Honey Makhija

Title : Modern Viking A Journey of Living by Ancient Values in a Contemporary World

Author : Honey Makhija

Edition : First (September, 2024)

ISBN : 9789348037701

Copyright © 2024, All Rights Reserved by Author

Published by

Regd. Add.: 254, Khuriyakhatta No. 10, Bindukhatta, Lalkuan, Nainital - 262402, Uttarakhand, India

Website : www.taneeshapublishers.in

E-mail : taneeshapublishers@gmail.com

Phone : +91 845481 2712, +91 976041 7980

Printed by :

Manipal Technologies Limited, Bengaluru - 560001, Karnataka

INDEX

Chapter - 1

Embrace Viking Values

Courage and Bravery: How Honey Faced Challenges in Business and Life

In the annals of history, the Vikings stand as paragons of courage and bravery, their tales echoing through time as legends of warriors who faced life with an unflinching spirit. They sailed across vast, unknown oceans, confronted fierce enemies, and braved the harshest elements, driven by a desire to explore, conquer, and thrive. Today, while the battles may be different, the need for courage remains as critical as ever. In the story of Honey Makhija, we find a modern embodiment of this Viking valor—an individual who has consistently demonstrated bravery not just in the face of external challenges, but in the internal battles that define one's true character.

Early Beginnings: The Spirit of Exploration

Honey Makhija's journey began in a middle-class family, where the seeds of his Viking-like spirit were sown early on. Raised with strong values and an emphasis on education, Honey was taught to be curious about the world, to ask questions, and to never be satisfied with easy answers. This early nurturing of his intellectual curiosity laid the foundation for a life characterized by a relentless pursuit of knowledge and success.

As he grew older, Honey's ambitions outpaced the boundaries of his hometown. He was drawn to the vibrant, multicultural hub of London—a city known for its opportunities, but also for its challenges. London is not for the faint of heart; it demands resilience, adaptability, and a willingness to face its fast-paced, often unforgiving nature. For Honey, moving to London was a courageous step into the unknown, much like the Vikings setting sail for distant shores.

Upon arriving in London, Honey immersed himself in his studies and later in the finance industry. It wasn't long before his talent, combined with his unyielding work ethic, began to pay off. By the age of 24, Honey had secured a prestigious position in a top financial firm, with an annual salary of 10 crores. For many, this would have been the pinnacle of success—a life of luxury in one of the world's greatest cities, financial security, and a promising career ahead.

The Call to Return: A Test of True Courage

But for Honey, something was missing. Despite the financial rewards and the vibrant life that London offered, he felt a growing disconnection from the values he held most dear. The fast-paced lifestyle, while exhilarating, left little room for the deep, meaningful connections that Honey cherished. The success he had achieved felt hollow without his family by his side.

It was at this juncture that Honey faced one of the most challenging decisions of his life. To stay in

London would have been the easier path—one that promised continued success, financial stability, and all the trappings of a prosperous career. But Honey knew that true courage is not about choosing the path of least resistance; it's about making the difficult decisions that align with one's core values.

In a move that many could not comprehend, Honey decided to leave his high-paying job and the life he had built in London to return to India. This decision was not driven by a lack of ambition or a desire to escape the pressures of his career. On the contrary, it was a testament to his courage—a decision to prioritize what truly mattered to him: his family.

Returning to India: Embracing New Challenges

Returning to India was not a retreat but a new beginning. Honey was determined to apply the knowledge and experience he had gained in London to build something meaningful in his homeland. He knew that the challenges would be different, but he was ready to face them with the same courage that had guided him throughout his life. Upon his return, Honey chose to venture into an industry that was entirely new to him—rice milling. Agriculture, and specifically rice milling, is a cornerstone of India's economy, but it is also a field fraught with challenges. The decision to enter this industry was driven by a combination of strategic thinking and a desire to contribute to a sector that had a direct impact on millions of lives.

Starting from scratch in the rice milling industry required not just business acumen but also an immense amount of courage.

Honey had to learn the intricacies of the industry, build relationships with farmers, navigate the complexities of supply chains, and manage the operational challenges of running a mill. These were uncharted waters for him, much like the Viking explorers who ventured into unknown territories.

But Honey's courage paid off. Not only did he

succeed in establishing his first rice mill, but he also expanded rapidly, opening two more factories within a short span of time. Each new factory was a testament to his vision, his willingness to take risks, and his ability to overcome the obstacles that came his way. In a country where the agricultural sector is often seen as fraught with difficulties, Honey's success was a beacon of what could be achieved with determination and bravery.

Venturing into Private Equity: A New Frontier

Having established a strong presence in the rice milling industry, Honey's ambitions did not stop there. He saw another opportunity—this time in the world of private equity. Private equity is a highly competitive field, requiring not only financial expertise but also the ability to identify and nurture potential in businesses. For Honey, this was not just a business venture; it was a way to expand his impact, to invest in companies that aligned with his values, and to contribute to their growth.

Opening his own family office in Mumbai was a significant step. It required not only the courage to invest his resources but also the vision to see opportunities where others might not. The decision to enter private equity was driven by the same Viking spirit that had guided Honey throughout his life—the courage to explore new frontiers and the determination to succeed.

As he built his family office, Honey focused on creating a portfolio that reflected his values of integrity, sustainability, and social impact. This approach set him apart in an industry that often prioritizes profit over principles. Honey's investments were not just about financial returns; they were about building businesses that would have a positive impact on society. This long-term vision, combined with his courageous approach to business, made Honey a respected figure in the private equity world.

Writing and Thought Leadership: A Courageous Voice

In addition to his business ventures, Honey found another outlet for his creativity and intellect—writing. By the age of 26, he had authored over ten books, covering a range of topics from business strategy to personal development. Writing is, in many ways, an act of bravery. It requires putting one's thoughts, ideas, and experiences into the public domain, exposing oneself to criticism, and engaging in the marketplace of ideas.

For Honey, writing was not just about sharing his knowledge; it was about contributing to the broader discourse on important issues. His books reflect his values, his experiences, and his belief in the power of ideas to change the world. Through his writing, Honey has inspired others to think critically, to challenge the status quo, and to approach life with the same courage that has guided his own journey.

In summary, Honey Makhija's life is a testament to the Viking value of courage. From leaving a lucrative career in London to venturing into new industries in India, to building a successful private equity firm and authoring multiple books, Honey has consistently demonstrated the bravery to face challenges, to make difficult decisions, and to live a life that aligns with his core values.

Honor and Integrity: A Strong Moral Code

Honor and integrity were the pillars of Viking society. The Vikings lived by a code of ethics that governed their actions and interactions, a code that was not enforced by law but by the collective conscience of the community. To break one's word was considered a grievous dishonor, and to live without integrity was to live without respect. In Honey Makhija's life, we see a modern embodiment of these ancient values—an unwavering commitment to honor and integrity that has defined his personal and professional life.

Business Ethics: The Foundation of Trust

In the business world, where competition is fierce and the temptation to cut corners is ever-present, maintaining one's integrity is not always easy. Yet, Honey has built his career on the foundation of trust, consistently prioritizing honesty and transparency over short-term gains. His approach to business is rooted in the belief that true success can only be achieved when it is built on a solid ethical foundation.

There have been numerous instances in Honey's career where he had to choose between profit and principle. In one notable example, Honey was involved in a high-stakes negotiation where the potential profits were enormous. However, the deal required him to compromise on certain ethical standards, something that Honey was not willing to do. Despite the pressure to go ahead with the deal, Honey chose to walk away, knowing that his reputation and integrity were worth more than any financial gain.

This decision was not without its consequences. Walking away from the deal meant losing out on a significant opportunity, and it was a decision that many in his position would have found difficult to make. However, for Honey, the choice was clear. He knew that compromising his integrity, even for a substantial profit, would have far-reaching implications—not just for his business, but for his personal values and the trust others placed in him.

Honey's commitment to integrity extends beyond his business dealings. In his philanthropic efforts, he is known for his transparency and accountability. Unlike many who use philanthropy as a means of enhancing their public image, Honey's charitable work is driven by a genuine desire to make a difference. He approaches his philanthropic projects with the same level of dedication and honesty that he brings to his business ventures, ensuring that every initiative is executed with integrity and that the intended beneficiaries receive the full impact of his efforts.

The Importance of Keeping One's Word

One of the most important aspects of honor is keeping one's word. For the Vikings, a person's word was binding, and breaking it was considered a serious breach of trust. Honey has lived by this principle throughout his life, understanding that trust is the most valuable currency in any relationship.

In business, Honey's word is his bond. Whether in negotiations, partnerships, or everyday interactions, those who work with Honey know that they can count on him to follow through on his commitments. This reliability has earned him a reputation for being someone who can be trusted, someone who will not waver when it comes to upholding his promises.

This commitment to keeping his word is not limited to major business deals; it extends to every aspect of his life. Honey believes that integrity is a habit, not an occasional practice. Whether it's a promise made to a colleague, a commitment to a community project, or a personal vow, Honey approaches every promise with the same level of seriousness. This consistency in honoring his commitments has not only strengthened his relationships but has also reinforced his own sense of self-respect and moral clarity.

Living with Integrity: A Personal Philosophy

For Honey, living with integrity is more than just a professional strategy—it is a personal philosophy that guides every decision he makes. Integrity, for Honey, is about being true to oneself and living in alignment with one's values. It's about making decisions that reflect who you are and what you stand for, even when no one is watching.

This philosophy has influenced every aspect of Honey's life, from his business ventures to his personal relationships. He understands that living with integrity requires constant self-reflection and a willingness to hold oneself accountable. It means being honest with oneself about one's motivations, being transparent in one's actions, and being consistent in one's values.

Honey's commitment to integrity has not always been easy. There have been times when living by his principles has meant facing criticism, losing opportunities, or enduring personal challenges. But through it all, Honey has remained steadfast in his belief that integrity is the foundation of a life well-lived. He knows that in the end, it is not the wealth he accumulates, the titles he holds, or the accolades he receives that will define his legacy—it is the integrity with which he has lived his life.

Philanthropy with Integrity

In the realm of philanthropy, Honey's commitment to integrity is equally evident. He has been involved in numerous charitable initiatives, ranging from education to healthcare to community development. What sets Honey's philanthropic efforts apart is his focus on ensuring that every project is executed with transparency and accountability.

Honey believes that philanthropy is not just about writing checks or donating money; it's about making a real, tangible impact on the lives of those who need it most. To this end, he is deeply involved in every project he undertakes, from the planning stages to the execution and follow-up. He works closely with his team to ensure that every initiative is aligned with his values of honesty and integrity, and that the intended beneficiaries receive the full benefits of the project.

This hands-on approach has not only ensured the success of Honey's philanthropic efforts but has also inspired others to approach philanthropy with the same level of dedication and integrity. By setting an example of how to give with integrity, Honey has contributed to a culture of transparency and accountability in the philanthropic world, demonstrating that true charity is about more than just giving—it's about giving with purpose and honor.

In summary, Honey Makhija's life is a testament to the Viking value of honor and integrity. From his business dealings to his philanthropic efforts, Honey has consistently lived by a code of ethics that prioritizes honesty, transparency, and accountability. His unwavering commitment to keeping his word, even at the cost of financial gain, reflects the Viking ideal of living with honor. In a world where integrity is often undervalued, Honey's life serves as a powerful reminder of the importance of living by one's principles and building a legacy of trust and respect.

Loyalty: A Commitment to Family and Community

Loyalty was the cornerstone of Viking society, where the bonds of kinship and community were sacred. The Vikings understood that their survival depended on the strength of their relationships, and they placed a high value on loyalty to family, friends, and allies. In Honey Makhija's life, this Viking value has been a guiding principle, shaping his decisions and defining his relationships.

Returning to India: A Profound Act of Loyalty

Honey's decision to leave London and return to India was not just a career move; it was a profound act of loyalty to his family. Despite the opportunities and success he had found in London,

Honey knew that his heart was with his family. For the Vikings, loyalty to one's kin was paramount, and Honey's decision to prioritize his family over his career is a modern reflection of this ancient value.

In London, Honey had built a life that many would envy—a successful career, financial stability, and the excitement of living in one of the world's greatest cities. But as much as he loved London, Honey knew that true fulfillment could only be found in the presence of those he loved. The decision to leave behind the life he had built in London was not an easy one, but it was a decision driven by his deep sense of loyalty to his family.

Returning to India meant starting over in many ways. It meant leaving behind the familiar and comfortable and embracing the unknown. But for Honey, the decision was clear. He knew that his family needed him, and he was willing to sacrifice his career and the life he had built in London to be with them. This act of loyalty is a testament to

Honey's character and his commitment to living by the values that matter most.

Building a Life in Mumbai: Loyalty to Community and Colleagues

Upon returning to India, Honey settled in Mumbai, a city known for its fast-paced lifestyle and bustling economy. Here, he quickly established himself as a force to be reckoned with in the business world. But even as he built his career in Mumbai, Honey never lost sight of the importance of loyalty—to his family, his community, and his colleagues.

In his businesses, Honey is known for his commitment to his employees and partners. He believes that loyalty is a two-way street—just as he expects loyalty from those who work with him, he is equally committed to being loyal to them. This means creating a supportive and inclusive work environment where everyone feels valued and respected.

Honey's approach to business is deeply rooted in

his belief that success is best achieved when it is shared. He understands that no one succeeds alone and that true success is the result of collective effort. By fostering a culture of loyalty and mutual support, Honey has built strong, lasting relationships with his colleagues and partners—relationships that have been instrumental in his success.

Leaving Mumbai: A Sacrifice for Family

After establishing himself in Mumbai and building a successful career, Honey once again made a significant life decision driven by loyalty. He chose to leave Mumbai, a city that had become the center of his business empire, to live closer to his family. This decision was not about abandoning his career or his ambitions; it was about integrating his professional success with his personal values.

For Honey, loyalty to his family has always been a priority. He understands that no matter how successful one becomes, true fulfillment can only be found in the presence of loved ones. By choosing to leave Mumbai and live closer to his family, Honey demonstrated that his loyalty to them outweighed the convenience and opportunities that the city offered. This decision was not without its challenges. Moving away from Mumbai meant restructuring his businesses and finding new ways to manage his operations. But Honey knew that being close to his family was worth any sacrifice. His decision to prioritize his family's well-being over his career is a modern reflection of the Viking value of loyalty, where the bonds of kinship were considered sacred.

Philanthropy: Loyalty to the Broader Community

Honey's sense of loyalty extends beyond his immediate family and colleagues to the broader community. He believes that with success comes a responsibility to give back, and he has made it a priority to contribute to the well-being of society through his philanthropic efforts.

Honey's approach to philanthropy is driven by a

deep sense of loyalty to the communities he serves. He understands that his success has been made possible by the support of others, and he is committed to giving back in meaningful ways. Whether it's through funding educational initiatives, supporting healthcare projects, or investing in community development, Honey's philanthropic efforts are a reflection of his loyalty to the broader community.

This loyalty is not just about financial contributions; it's about being present and actively involved in the causes he supports. Honey is known for his hands-on approach to philanthropy, working closely with his team and community leaders to ensure that every project is executed with care and integrity. His commitment to making a positive impact on society is a testament to his loyalty to the communities that have supported him throughout his journey.

Creating a Legacy of Loyalty

For Honey, loyalty is not just a value; it's a way of

life. It's about being true to oneself and to those who matter most. It's about building relationships based on trust, respect, and mutual support. And it's about creating a legacy that reflects the values that have guided him throughout his life.

Honey's legacy of loyalty is evident in the strong relationships he has built with his family, colleagues, and community. It's evident in the success of his businesses, which have thrived not just because of his leadership but because of the loyalty and dedication of those who work with him. And it's evident in the positive impact he has made on society through his philanthropic efforts.

In a world where loyalty is often undervalued, Honey's life serves as a powerful reminder of the importance of staying true to one's values and to the people who matter most. His commitment to loyalty, whether to his family, his colleagues, or his community, is a reflection of the Viking ideal of kinship—a value that is just as relevant today as it was in ancient times.

Conclusion

In embracing Viking values, Honey Makhija has not only achieved remarkable success but has done so in a way that honors the principles of courage, honor, and loyalty. His journey from London to India, from finance to rice milling to private equity, and his commitment to family and community, all reflect the timeless relevance of these ancient values. Honey's life is a modern-day testament to the power of living with purpose and integrity, proving that the Viking spirit is not just a relic of the past but a guiding light for the present and future.

Chapter - 2

Physical Strength and Fitness

The Vikings were known for their extraordinary physical strength and endurance, traits that were essential for their survival in the harsh Scandinavian environment. Their lives were a constant battle against the elements, as well as against their enemies. Physical prowess was not just admired but necessary, as it enabled them to navigate treacherous seas, engage in brutal combat, and endure the demanding physical labor required in their daily lives. In modern times, while we may not face the same physical challenges, the principles of physical strength, fitness, and a connection with nature remain as relevant as ever. Honey Makhija's commitment to these principles is a testament to the enduring power of the Viking way of life.

Exercise Regularly: A Commitment to Physical Fitness

In the modern world, where the demands of work and life often lead to a sedentary lifestyle, maintaining physical fitness requires dedication and discipline. For Honey Makhija, this commitment to physical fitness is not just a routine; it is a way of life, inspired by the Viking belief in the importance of strength and resilience.

The Importance of Physical Fitness

From a young age, Honey understood the value of physical fitness. He recognized that a strong body was not only essential for maintaining health but also for achieving success in all areas of life. Just as the Vikings relied on their physical strength to navigate the challenges of their world, Honey knew that maintaining his physical fitness would be crucial in helping him navigate the demands of his own life.

Honey's approach to fitness is rooted in the belief

that the body is a temple that must be cared for and respected. He understands that physical fitness is not just about looking good; it's about feeling strong, confident, and capable. It's about having the energy and endurance to pursue one's goals and live life to the fullest. For Honey, physical fitness is a foundation upon which all other aspects of life are built.

A Daily Routine Inspired by the Vikings

Honey's commitment to physical fitness is evident in his daily routine, which is inspired by the Vikings' emphasis on strength and endurance. Each day begins with a rigorous workout that includes a combination of strength training, cardiovascular exercise, and flexibility work. This routine is designed to build and maintain the physical strength that is essential for both his professional and personal life.

Strength training is a core component of Honey's fitness regimen. He understands that building muscle is not just about aesthetics; it's about developing the power and resilience needed to tackle the challenges of life. Honey incorporates weightlifting into his daily routine, focusing on compound exercises such as squats, deadlifts, and bench presses—movements that engage multiple muscle groups and build functional strength. These exercises are reminiscent of the physical demands placed on the Vikings, who needed to be strong enough to carry heavy loads, row long distances, and wield weapons in battle.

In addition to strength training, Honey includes cardiovascular exercise in his routine to build endurance and maintain cardiovascular health. This may include running, cycling, or rowing—activities that not only improve heart health but also mirror the Vikings' physical activities, such as rowing longboats across the open sea or running across rugged terrain during raids. Cardiovascular fitness is essential for maintaining the stamina required to keep up with the demands of a busy life, and Honey ensures that his routine includes activities that challenge his endurance.

Flexibility and mobility are also important aspects of Honey's fitness regimen. He incorporates stretching and yoga into his daily routine to improve flexibility, reduce the risk of injury, and enhance overall physical performance. Flexibility is often overlooked in fitness routines, but Honey understands that it is essential for maintaining a balanced and healthy body. By incorporating stretching and yoga, Honey ensures that his body remains agile and adaptable—qualities that were also valued by the Vikings, who needed to be nimble and quick in combat.

The Mental Benefits of Physical Fitness

Honey's commitment to physical fitness is not just about the physical benefits; it's also about the mental and emotional benefits that come with regular exercise. Physical fitness has been shown to improve mental clarity, reduce stress, and enhance mood—all of which are essential for maintaining a positive and focused mindset.

For Honey, exercise is a form of meditation. It is a time when he can clear his mind, focus on his breathing, and connect with his body. The repetitive movements of strength training, the rhythmic pace of running, and the controlled breathing of yoga all serve to calm the mind and bring a sense of peace and clarity. This mental clarity is essential for Honey as he navigates the complexities of his business and personal life.

Exercise also provides Honey with a sense of accomplishment. Each workout is a challenge, and completing it gives him a feeling of achievement that sets a positive tone for the rest of the day. This sense of accomplishment is important for building confidence and self-esteem, which are essential qualities for success in any endeavor. By starting his day with a challenging workout, Honey sets the tone for the rest of the day, approaching his tasks with a sense of determination and confidence.

Balancing Physical Fitness with a Busy Schedule

One of the biggest challenges for many people when it comes to maintaining physical fitness is finding the time to exercise. Between work, family, and other responsibilities, it can be difficult to prioritize fitness. However, Honey has found a way to balance his busy schedule with his commitment to physical fitness.

Honey's approach to balancing fitness with his schedule is rooted in the Viking principle of discipline. Just as the Vikings were disciplined in their training and preparation for battle, Honey is disciplined in his approach to fitness. He treats his workouts as non-negotiable appointments in his calendar, making them a priority even when life gets busy. This discipline ensures that he stays consistent with his fitness routine, regardless of the demands of his schedule.

Honey also understands the importance of flexibility when it comes to fitness. While he maintains a consistent routine, he is also willing to adapt his workouts based on his schedule and energy levels. If he has a particularly busy day, he may opt for a shorter, high-intensity workout that still provides the benefits of exercise without taking up too much time. On days when he has more time, he may engage in longer, more leisurely activities such as hiking or swimming. This flexibility allows Honey to stay committed to his fitness goals while also accommodating the demands of his life.

The Long-Term Benefits of Physical Fitness

Honey's commitment to physical fitness is not just about short-term gains; it's about building a strong foundation for long-term health and well-being. He understands that the benefits of regular exercise extend far beyond the immediate effects, and that maintaining physical fitness is essential for living a long, healthy, and fulfilling life.

Physical fitness has been shown to reduce the risk of chronic diseases such as heart disease, diabetes, and obesity—conditions that are prevalent in today's society. By maintaining a regular exercise routine, Honey is taking proactive steps to protect his health and ensure that he remains strong and capable well into old age. This long-term approach to fitness is a reflection of the Viking belief in the importance of preparation and resilience. Just as the Vikings prepared for long voyages and harsh winters, Honey is preparing for the future by taking care of his body today.

In addition to the physical health benefits, Honey also recognizes the impact that fitness has on his mental and emotional well-being. Regular exercise has been shown to reduce the risk of depression and anxiety, improve cognitive function, and enhance overall quality of life. By staying physically active, Honey is not only ensuring that he remains healthy and strong, but he is also investing in his mental and emotional well-being.

Inspiring Others Through Fitness

Honey's commitment to physical fitness has not

only benefited his own life, but it has also inspired others to prioritize their health and well-being. Through his example, Honey has shown that it is possible to maintain a high level of physical fitness even in the midst of a busy and demanding life.

Honey often shares his fitness journey with others, whether through social media, speaking engagements, or personal conversations. He encourages others to take charge of their health and to make fitness a priority in their own lives. Honey's approach is not about perfection; it's about consistency and effort. He understands that everyone's fitness journey is unique, and he encourages others to find what works best for them and to stay committed to their goals.

By sharing his own fitness journey, Honey has inspired many to take the first step toward a healthier lifestyle. Whether it's starting a new workout routine, making healthier food choices, or simply taking the time to be more active, Honey's example has motivated others to make positive changes in their lives.

In summary, Honey Makhija's commitment to physical fitness is a modern reflection of the Viking value of strength and resilience. Through a disciplined and consistent approach to exercise, Honey has built a strong foundation for his physical, mental, and emotional well-being. His daily routine, inspired by the Vikings, has not only benefited his own life but has also inspired others to prioritize their health and fitness. In a world where physical fitness is often neglected, Honey's dedication serves as a powerful reminder of the importance of taking care of one's body and mind.

Connect with Nature: Balancing Business with Time Spent in Nature

The Vikings had a profound connection with the natural world. They revered the elements—earth, water, air, and fire—understanding that their survival depended on living in harmony with nature. Whether it was sailing across the open seas, farming the land, or enduring the harsh winters, the Vikings knew that their fate was intertwined with the forces of nature. In today's world, where technology often distances us from the natural environment, maintaining a connection with nature is more important than ever. Honey Makhija's approach to balancing his business life with time spent in nature is a testament to the enduring relevance of the Viking connection to the natural world.

The Healing Power of Nature

Honey has always been drawn to nature. From a young age, he felt a deep sense of peace and contentment when surrounded by the natural world. Whether it was walking through the forests, swimming in the ocean, or simply sitting by a river, Honey found that nature provided a respite from the demands of daily life and a source of inspiration and renewal.

As he grew older and his responsibilities increased, Honey recognized the importance of maintaining his connection with nature. He understood that spending time in nature was not just a luxury; it was a necessity for his overall well-being. Just as the Vikings found solace and strength in the natural world, Honey discovered that nature had the power to heal, to restore, and to provide perspective.

The healing power of nature is well-documented. Studies have shown that spending time in nature can reduce stress, lower blood pressure, improve mood, and enhance cognitive function. For Honey, these benefits are not just theoretical; they are an integral part of his life. He makes it a priority to spend time in nature regularly, knowing that it helps him to stay grounded, focused, and balanced.

Hiking: A Modern-Day Viking Adventure

One of the ways Honey connects with nature is through hiking. Hiking allows him to experience the beauty and majesty of the natural world while also providing a physical challenge that keeps him fit and strong. For Honey, hiking is more than just a recreational activity; it is a way to reconnect with his Viking roots and to experience the world in a way that is both physically and mentally rewarding.

Hiking through mountains, forests, and along coastal paths, Honey finds that each hike is a journey of discovery. Just as the Vikings explored new lands and territories, Honey explores the natural world, finding joy in the simple act of putting one foot in front of the other. The physical exertion of hiking, combined with the serenity of nature, provides Honey with a sense of accomplishment and peace that is difficult to find in the modern world.

Hiking also allows Honey to disconnect from the constant stimulation of modern life. In the quiet of the mountains or the solitude of a forest, he is free from the distractions of technology, the demands of business, and the noise of the city. This time in nature allows Honey to reflect, to clear his mind, and to gain perspective on the challenges he faces in his daily life.

Retreats: Recharging in Nature

In addition to regular hikes, Honey also makes it a point to take extended retreats in nature. These retreats are an opportunity for him to completely disconnect from his business life and to immerse himself in the natural world. Whether it's a week spent in a remote cabin in the mountains, a meditation retreat in the forest, or a coastal getaway, Honey uses these retreats as a time to recharge and to reconnect with what is truly important.

During these retreats, Honey engages in a variety of activities that allow him to fully experience the beauty and power of nature. He may spend his days hiking, swimming, or kayaking, and his evenings sitting by a campfire, watching the stars, or simply enjoying the sounds of the natural world. These retreats provide Honey with the space and time he needs to reflect on his life, to set intentions for the future, and to gain clarity on the decisions he needs to make.

These retreats are not just a break from the demands of business; they are a vital part of Honey's approach to life. He understands that in order to be effective in his work and to maintain his physical and mental health, he needs to regularly step away from the pressures of daily life and to reconnect with the natural world. Just as the Vikings took time to honor the forces of nature and to prepare for the challenges ahead, Honey uses these retreats to recharge his energy, to clear his mind, and to prepare for the tasks that lie ahead.

Nature as a Source of Inspiration

For Honey, nature is not just a place to relax; it is also a source of inspiration. Many of his best ideas and insights have come to him while spending time in nature. The beauty, simplicity, and power of the natural world provide Honey with a fresh perspective on the challenges he faces in his business and personal life.

Whether it's the patience required to navigate a winding mountain trail, the resilience of a tree growing in harsh conditions, or the persistence of a river carving its way through rock, Honey finds that nature is full of lessons that can be applied to his own life. These observations provide him with valuable insights into how to approach challenges, how to stay focused on his goals, and how to remain resilient in the face of adversity.

Honey also finds that nature inspires his creativity. As a writer, he often finds that the peace and solitude of nature provide the perfect environment for generating new ideas and for reflecting on the themes he wishes to explore in his work. Many of his books have been written during or after his time spent in nature, and he credits these experiences with providing him with the clarity and focus needed to produce his best work.

Balancing Business with Time in Nature

One of the challenges that many people face when it comes to spending time in nature is finding the time to do so. Between work, family, and other responsibilities, it can be difficult to prioritize time in the natural world. However, Honey has found a way to balance his demanding business life with his commitment to spending time in nature.

Honey's approach to balancing business with time in nature is rooted in the belief that time in nature is essential for maintaining overall well-being. Just as he prioritizes physical fitness, Honey also prioritizes time in nature, understanding that it is an integral part of his overall health and success.

To ensure that he has time to connect with nature, Honey schedules it into his calendar just as he would any other important meeting or appointment. He makes it a priority to get outside every day, whether it's for a morning walk, an afternoon hike, or a weekend retreat. By treating time in nature as a non-negotiable part of his routine, Honey ensures that he stays connected with the natural world, even when life gets busy.

Honey also looks for opportunities to incorporate

nature into his daily routine. Whether it's taking a walk during a lunch break, having a meeting in a park, or simply opening a window to let in fresh air, Honey finds ways to bring the natural world into his everyday life. This approach allows him to maintain his connection with nature, even on the busiest of days.

Teaching Others to Connect with Nature

Honey's commitment to nature has not only benefited his own life but has also inspired others to reconnect with the natural world. He often shares his experiences in nature with others, whether through social media, speaking engagements, or personal conversations. He encourages others to take the time to connect with nature, understanding that it is essential for maintaining overall well-being.

Honey also organizes retreats and outdoor experiences for his colleagues, friends, and family. These retreats provide an opportunity for others to experience the healing and restorative power of nature, and to gain a deeper appreciation for the natural world. Through these experiences, Honey hopes to inspire others to make nature a regular part of their lives, and to understand the importance of living in harmony with the environment.

Nature as a Reflection of the Viking Spirit

Honey's connection with nature is a modern reflection of the Viking spirit. Just as the Vikings revered the natural world and understood the importance of living in harmony with the elements, Honey recognizes that his success and well-being are closely tied to his relationship with nature. He understands that just as the Vikings depended on the land and sea for their survival, he too depends on nature for his physical, mental, and emotional health.

By making time for nature in his life, Honey is honoring the Viking tradition of living in harmony with the environment. He is also ensuring that he remains grounded, focused, and balanced, even in the midst of a busy and demanding life. Just as the Vikings found strength, resilience, and inspiration in the natural world, Honey finds that nature provides him with the clarity, perspective, and energy needed to live a fulfilling and successful life.

Conclusion

Honey Makhija's commitment to physical fitness and his connection with nature are modern reflections of the Viking values of strength, resilience, and harmony with the environment. Through a disciplined and consistent approach to fitness, Honey has built a strong foundation for his physical, mental, and emotional well-being. His daily routine, inspired by the Vikings, has not only benefited his own life but has also inspired others to prioritize their health and fitness.

In addition to his commitment to physical fitness, Honey's deep connection with nature has provided him with a source of inspiration, healing, and perspective. By making time for nature in his life, Honey is honoring the Viking tradition of living in harmony with the environment, and he is ensuring that he remains grounded and focused, even in the midst of a busy and demanding life.

Through his dedication to physical fitness and his connection with nature, Honey Makhija has demonstrated that the Viking values of strength, resilience, and harmony with the environment are just as relevant today as they were in ancient times. By embracing these values, Honey has created a life that is not only successful and fulfilling but also deeply connected to the natural world and to the principles that have guided him throughout his journey.

Chapter - 3

Simplicity and Minimalism

In an age where the demands of modern life often lead to a cluttered existence, both physically and mentally, the ancient Viking principle of simplicity holds profound relevance. The Vikings, despite their legendary exploits and complex social structures, lived lives that were deeply rooted in simplicity and minimalism. Their approach to life was one of necessity, dictated by the harsh environments they inhabited, yet it fostered a focus on what truly mattered: survival, honor, community, and craftsmanship. In a similar vein, Honey Makhija has embraced these values in his modern life, consciously choosing a path of simplicity and minimalism that allows him to focus on what is truly important.

Minimalist Living: Focusing on What Truly Matters

Minimalism, as a lifestyle choice, has gained significant attention in recent years, often presented as an antidote to the overwhelming consumerism that characterizes much of modern society. At its core, minimalism is about stripping away the excess to focus on what truly matters. It's about making deliberate choices that prioritize quality over quantity, clarity over chaos, and intentionality over mindlessness. For Honey Makhija, minimalism is not just a trend; it is a way of life that allows him to maintain focus, clarity, and purpose in everything he does.

The Philosophy of Minimalism

Honey's journey into minimalism began with a realization that the relentless pursuit of material wealth and the accumulation of possessions were not bringing him the fulfillment he sought. Despite his success in business and his ability to afford a life of luxury, Honey found that the more he acquired, the more cluttered and distracted his life became. He realized that the constant drive for more was pulling him away from the things that truly mattered—his relationships, his health, his passions, and his sense of purpose.

Inspired by the simplicity of the Viking lifestyle, Honey began to embrace the principles of minimalism. He understood that the Vikings lived with few possessions, not out of choice but out of necessity. Yet, this simplicity allowed them to focus on what was truly important: their survival, their community, and their values. For Honey, minimalism became a way to recenter his life, to strip away the unnecessary distractions, and to focus on what truly mattered.

Minimalism, as Honey practices it, is not about deprivation or asceticism. It is about making intentional choices that align with one's values and priorities. It is about recognizing that more is not always better, and that true fulfillment comes from living in alignment with one's purpose, rather than from accumulating material possessions. Honey's approach to minimalism is deeply personal and reflects his commitment to living a life of purpose, clarity, and intention.

Decluttering: A Path to Clarity

One of the first steps Honey took in his minimalist journey was to declutter his physical space. He realized that his home, office, and even his digital life were filled with things that did not add value to his life. These things, whether they were physical objects, digital files, or even commitments and obligations, were creating noise and distraction, pulling him away from what was truly important.

Decluttering, for Honey, was not just about getting rid of things; it was about creating space— space for clarity, space for creativity, and space for the things that truly mattered. He approached decluttering with the same discipline and intentionality that he applied to other areas of his life. Each item, each commitment, each piece of information was carefully considered. If it did not add value or serve a purpose, it was removed.

This process was not easy. It required Honey to confront his attachment to material possessions, to recognize the ways in which he had been using things to fill voids or to distract himself from deeper issues. But as he let go of the unnecessary, he found that he gained something far more valuable: clarity. With less clutter in his life, Honey found that he had more mental and emotional space to focus on what truly mattered. He was able to think more clearly, to make better decisions, and to engage more fully with the people and activities that were most important to him.

Living with Intentionality

Minimalism, as Honey practices it, is not just about decluttering; it is about living with intentionality. It is about making deliberate choices that reflect one's values and priorities. For Honey, this means being intentional about how he spends his time, energy, and resources.

One of the ways Honey practices intentionality is

by carefully curating his daily routines and habits. He understands that habits are the building blocks of life, and that by choosing the right habits, he can create a life that is aligned with his values. Honey's daily routine is simple but effective. It includes time for exercise, reflection, work, and connection with loved ones. Each part of his routine is chosen with intention, designed to support his physical, mental, and emotional well-being.

Honey also applies this principle of intentionality to his relationships. He understands that the quality of his relationships has a profound impact on his overall happiness and fulfillment. As a result, he is intentional about the people he surrounds himself with, choosing to spend time with those who uplift, support, and inspire him. This means saying no to relationships that are draining or toxic, and investing in those that bring joy and meaning to his life.

In his work, Honey is equally intentional. He focuses on projects and initiatives that align with his values and that have a positive impact on the world. He is careful not to take on too many commitments, recognizing that spreading himself too thin would dilute his effectiveness and pull him away from what truly matters. By being intentional about his work, Honey is able to maintain a sense of purpose and fulfillment, even in the midst of a busy and demanding career.

The Power of Saying No

A key aspect of Honey's minimalist approach to life is his ability to say no. In a world where opportunities and demands are constantly vying for attention, the ability to say no is a powerful tool for maintaining focus and clarity. For Honey, saying no is not about rejecting opportunities or being closed off to new experiences; it is about protecting his time, energy, and resources so that he can focus on what truly matters.

Honey recognizes that every yes comes with a cost. Saying yes to one thing means saying no to something else, and if he is not careful, he could end up saying yes to things that do not align with his values or priorities. To avoid this, Honey practices what he calls "purposeful noes." These are deliberate decisions to decline opportunities, invitations, or commitments that do not serve his higher purpose.

This practice has allowed Honey to maintain a clear focus on his goals and to ensure that his time and energy are directed toward the things that matter most. It has also given him the freedom to pursue his passions and to engage in activities that bring him joy and fulfillment. By saying no to the unnecessary, Honey has created space in his life for what truly matters.

Living with Less: The Benefits of Minimalism

As Honey embraced minimalism, he discovered that living with less brought a host of benefits. One of the most immediate benefits was a sense of freedom. With fewer possessions and fewer commitments, Honey found that he had more time, energy, and resources to devote to the things that truly mattered. He was no longer weighed down by the burden of maintaining and managing an excess of things, and this allowed him to live with greater ease and simplicity.

Another benefit of minimalism was an increased sense of clarity and focus. With less clutter in his life, Honey found that he was able to think more clearly and make better decisions. He was no longer distracted by the noise and chaos of excess, and this allowed him to stay focused on his goals and priorities. This clarity and focus have been instrumental in helping Honey achieve success in both his personal and professional life.

Minimalism also brought Honey a greater sense of contentment and satisfaction. By focusing on what truly mattered, he found that he was able to derive more joy and fulfillment from the simple things in life. He no longer felt the need to chase after material possessions or to constantly seek more. Instead, he found contentment in living in alignment with his values and in being present to the people and experiences that brought him joy.

Minimalism in Business: A Focus on Quality and Impact

Honey's minimalist approach to life extends to his business practices as well. In a world where businesses often prioritize growth at all costs, Honey has chosen a different path. He believes that success in business is not just about scale or profit; it's about quality, impact, and sustainability. This philosophy is deeply rooted in the Viking principle of craftsmanship, where quality and excellence were valued above all else.

In his businesses, Honey applies the principles of minimalism by focusing on what truly matters: delivering value, maintaining quality, and creating a positive impact. He is deliberate in his choice of projects, ensuring that each one aligns with his values and has the potential to make a meaningful difference. This focus on quality over quantity has allowed Honey to build a reputation for excellence and to create businesses that are not only successful but also sustainable.

One of the ways Honey practices minimalism in his business is by streamlining operations and reducing waste. He understands that efficiency is key to maintaining quality, and that by eliminating unnecessary processes, he can focus on delivering the best possible product or service. This approach is reminiscent of the Viking way of life, where efficiency and resourcefulness were essential for survival.

Honey also applies minimalism to his leadership style. He believes that effective leadership is about clarity, focus, and simplicity. He is intentional in his communication, ensuring that his messages are clear and concise, and that his team understands the goals and priorities of the business. This clarity allows his team to stay focused on what truly matters and to work together toward a common goal.

The Role of Minimalism in Personal Fulfillment

For Honey, minimalism is not just a tool for achieving success in business; it is also a path to personal fulfillment. By stripping away the excess and focusing on what truly matters, Honey has been able to create a life that is aligned with his values and that brings him a deep sense of contentment and satisfaction.

One of the key aspects of personal fulfillment for Honey is the ability to live in alignment with his values. Minimalism has allowed him to do this by creating space for the things that truly matter to him. Whether it's spending time with loved ones, pursuing his passions, or giving back to the community, Honey's minimalist lifestyle allows him to live in a way that is true to who he is and what he believes in.

Another aspect of personal fulfillment for Honey is the ability to be present and engaged in the moment. By removing the distractions and clutter from his life, Honey has been able to cultivate a greater sense of mindfulness and presence. He is able to fully engage in the activities and relationships that bring him joy, and this has had a profound impact on his overall well-being.

Honey also finds personal fulfillment in the simplicity and ease that minimalism brings. By living with less, he has been able to reduce the stress and complexity in his life, and this has allowed him to experience greater peace and contentment. He no longer feels the need to chase after more, and this has given him the freedom to focus on what truly matters.

Craftsmanship: A Hands-On Approach to Quality and Excellence

The Vikings were renowned for their craftsmanship. Whether it was in the construction of their longboats, the forging of their weapons, or the creation of their art, the Vikings approached their work with a commitment to quality and excellence. This dedication to craftsmanship was not just about creating functional objects; it was about creating something of lasting value, something that reflected the skill, pride, and integrity of the maker. In his own life, Honey Makhija has embraced this principle of craftsmanship, applying it to his businesses, his personal projects, and his approach to life.

The Importance of Craftsmanship

For Honey, craftsmanship is about more than just creating a high-quality product or service; it is about taking pride in one's work and striving for excellence in everything one does. He believes that craftsmanship is a reflection of one's values and that the care and attention one puts into their work is a testament to their character.

In his businesses, Honey applies the principles of craftsmanship by focusing on quality and attention to detail. He understands that in order to create something of lasting value, one must be willing to invest the time, effort, and resources needed to do it right. This commitment to quality is evident in every aspect of his work, from the products and services he delivers to the relationships he builds with his clients and partners.

Honey also believes that craftsmanship is about continuous improvement. Just as the Vikings constantly refined their techniques and improved their tools, Honey is always looking for ways to enhance the quality of his work. He is committed to learning, growing, and evolving, and he encourages his team to do the same. This dedication to continuous improvement ensures that Honey's businesses remain at the forefront of their industries and that they continue to deliver value to their clients.

A Hands-On Approach

One of the key aspects of Honey's approach to craftsmanship is his hands-on involvement in his businesses. Unlike some leaders who delegate tasks and remain at a distance, Honey believes in being actively involved in the work. He takes a hands-on approach to everything he does, from the strategic planning of his businesses to the day-to-day operations.

This hands-on approach allows Honey to ensure that every aspect of his businesses meets his high standards of quality. He is not content to simply oversee the work; he wants to be involved in the process, to understand the details, and to contribute his expertise. This level of involvement not only ensures that the work is done right but also sets an example for his team, showing them the importance of taking pride in their work and striving for excellence.

Honey's hands-on approach is also a reflection of his belief in the value of hard work. He understands that craftsmanship is not just about talent or skill; it is about dedication, perseverance, and a willingness to put in the effort needed to achieve excellence. By being actively involved in his work, Honey demonstrates his commitment to these values and inspires his team to do the same.

Craftsmanship in Personal Projects

In addition to his businesses, Honey applies the principles of craftsmanship to his personal projects as well. Whether it's writing a book, building a piece of furniture, or creating a work of art, Honey approaches each project with the same level of care, attention to detail, and commitment to quality.

For Honey, these personal projects are not just hobbies; they are an expression of his values and a way to cultivate his creativity and skill. He believes that engaging in hands-on work is essential for maintaining a connection to one's craft and for continuing to grow and develop as a person.

One of the ways Honey practices craftsmanship in his personal projects is by focusing on the process rather than the outcome. He understands that the true value of craftsmanship lies in the journey, in the act of creating something with care and intention. By focusing on the process, Honey is able to fully engage with his work, to learn from his mistakes, and to continuously improve his skills.

This focus on the process also allows Honey to find joy and fulfillment in his work. He understands that craftsmanship is not just about the end result; it is about the satisfaction that comes from creating something with one's own hands, from knowing that every detail has been carefully considered and executed with care. This sense of satisfaction and pride in one's work is a key aspect of Honey's approach to craftsmanship, and it is something that he strives to cultivate in all areas of his life.

Craftsmanship in Leadership

Honey also applies the principles of craftsmanship to his leadership style. He believes that effective leadership is about more than just making decisions or giving orders; it is about setting an example, guiding and mentoring others, and creating an environment where quality and excellence are valued and pursued.

As a leader, Honey is deeply involved in the development of his team. He takes the time to mentor and coach his employees, helping them to develop their skills and to take pride in their work. He encourages them to approach their work with the same level of care and attention to detail that he applies to his own work, and he supports them in their pursuit of excellence.

Honey's leadership style is also characterized by a commitment to continuous improvement. He understands that in order to create a culture of craftsmanship, he must be willing to invest in the development of his team and to provide them with the resources and support they need to succeed. This commitment to continuous improvement ensures that Honey's businesses remain competitive and that his team continues to grow and evolve.

The Legacy of Craftsmanship

For Honey, craftsmanship is not just about achieving success in the present; it is about creating a legacy that will endure. He believes that the work he does today is a reflection of his character and values, and that it will leave a lasting impact on the world.

Honey's commitment to craftsmanship is evident

in the quality of the products and services his businesses deliver, in the relationships he builds with his clients and partners, and in the impact he has on his team and the community. By focusing on quality, attention to detail, and continuous improvement, Honey is creating a legacy of excellence that will stand the test of time.

This legacy is not just about the tangible products and services Honey creates; it is about the values and principles he instills in others. By setting an example of craftsmanship, Honey is inspiring others to take pride in their work, to strive for excellence, and to approach their work with care and intention. This is the true legacy of craftsmanship—a legacy that goes beyond the physical and leaves a lasting impact on the world.

Conclusion

Honey Makhija's approach to simplicity and minimalism is a modern reflection of the Viking values of focus, clarity, and craftsmanship. Through his commitment to minimalist living, Honey has created a life that is aligned with his values and that brings him a deep sense of contentment and fulfillment. By stripping away the excess and focusing on what truly matters, Honey has been able to maintain clarity, focus, and purpose in everything he does.

In addition to his minimalist approach to life, Honey's commitment to craftsmanship is evident in every aspect of his work. Whether in his businesses, his personal projects, or his leadership, Honey approaches everything he does with a focus on quality, attention to detail, and a commitment to continuous improvement. This dedication to craftsmanship is a reflection of Honey's values and a testament to his belief in the importance of creating something of lasting value.

Through his dedication to simplicity, minimalism, and craftsmanship, Honey Makhija has created a life that is not only successful and fulfilling but also deeply connected to the values and principles that have guided him throughout his journey. In a world where complexity, distraction, and excess often reign, Honey's approach serves as a powerful reminder of the importance of living with intentionality, focus, and care.

Chapter - 4

Diet and Nutrition

The diet of the Vikings, rooted in the rugged environment of Scandinavia, was essential for their survival and strength. Although the Vikings were known for their consumption of meat and fish, the core principles of their diet—emphasizing whole, natural foods and a balanced approach to eating—are universally applicable, even in a vegetarian context. Honey Makhija, while following a vegetarian lifestyle, has adapted these principles to create a diet that nourishes both body and mind. His approach to diet and nutrition reflects a modern interpretation of the Viking way, focusing on whole foods, sustainability, and a balanced practice of feasting and fasting.

Eat Like a Viking: Emphasizing Whole Foods and Natural Ingredients in a Vegetarian Diet

The Viking diet, while traditionally rich in meat

and fish, was also heavily reliant on whole grains, vegetables, and dairy products, particularly in the more agriculturally productive regions. These elements of the diet, rooted in natural, unprocessed foods, align closely with the principles of a modern vegetarian diet. Honey Makhija's approach to eating, which prioritizes these whole foods and natural ingredients, mirrors the Viking emphasis on consuming what the earth provides in its most unaltered form.

The Foundation of a Vegetarian Viking-Inspired Diet

Honey's vegetarian diet is centered around the same principles that guided the Vikings: simplicity, sustainability, and nourishment. He focuses on consuming foods that are minimally processed, locally sourced, and rich in nutrients. This includes a wide variety of vegetables, whole grains, legumes, nuts, seeds, and dairy products, all of which provide the essential nutrients needed to maintain his health and vitality.

For Honey, the emphasis is on quality and variety. He understands that a well-rounded vegetarian diet must include a diverse range of foods to ensure that all nutritional needs are met. This variety not only supports his physical health but also keeps his meals interesting and enjoyable, much like the varied diet of the Vikings, who relied on seasonal and local foods.

Protein-Rich Plant Foods: The Viking Staple Reimagined

While the Vikings consumed animal protein as a staple of their diet, Honey sources his protein from plant-based foods. Protein is essential for building and maintaining muscle, supporting metabolic functions, and providing sustained energy. Honey's diet includes a variety of plant-based proteins such as lentils, chickpeas, black beans, tofu, tempeh, and quinoa. These foods are rich in essential amino acids and provide the building blocks necessary for maintaining strength and health.

Honey also incorporates nuts and seeds into his

diet as additional sources of protein and healthy fats. Almonds, walnuts, chia seeds, and flaxseeds not only contribute to his protein intake but also provide omega-3 fatty acids, which are important for heart health and cognitive function. By focusing on these nutrient-dense plant foods, Honey ensures that his vegetarian diet supports his active lifestyle, much like the protein-rich diet of the Vikings.

In addition to the direct sources of protein, Honey also emphasizes the importance of complementary proteins—combining different plant-based foods to ensure he gets all the essential amino acids his body needs. For instance, pairing beans with rice or whole grains with legumes creates complete protein profiles, mirroring the balanced approach of the Viking diet, albeit in a plant-based context.

Whole Grains and Vegetables: The Core of the Vegetarian Diet

Whole grains and vegetables were vital components of the Viking diet, providing essential nutrients and energy. For Honey, these foods form the core of his vegetarian diet, offering a wide range of vitamins, minerals, and fiber that support overall health and well-being.

Honey includes a variety of whole grains in his meals, such as quinoa, brown rice, barley, oats, and millet. These grains are not only rich in complex carbohydrates, which provide sustained energy, but also contain important nutrients like B vitamins, iron, and magnesium. By incorporating a variety of whole grains, Honey ensures that his diet remains balanced and nutrient-dense.

Vegetables are another key component of Honey's diet, providing a rich source of vitamins, minerals, and antioxidants. He makes it a priority to include a colorful array of vegetables in his meals, ranging from leafy greens like spinach and kale to cruciferous vegetables like broccoli and cauliflower, and root vegetables like carrots and sweet potatoes. These vegetables not only enhance the nutritional value of his diet but also add variety and flavor, much like the diverse plant foods consumed by the Vikings.

Honey is particularly mindful of including seasonal and locally grown vegetables in his diet. This not only supports local agriculture but also ensures that he is consuming foods at their peak nutritional value, a practice that aligns with the Viking approach to eating what the land provides.

Dairy and Fermented Foods: A Source of Vital Nutrients

The Vikings consumed dairy products like milk, cheese, and yogurt as important sources of nutrition, particularly in regions where farming was prominent. Similarly, Honey includes dairy products in his vegetarian diet, recognizing their value as sources of protein, calcium, and probiotics, which are essential for bone health, digestion, and overall well-being.

Honey consumes a variety of dairy products, including Greek yogurt, kefir, and paneer, which are rich in protein and calcium. These foods also provide probiotics, which support a healthy gut microbiome—an essential aspect of overall health. By incorporating these nutrient-rich dairy products into his diet, Honey mirrors the Viking practice of consuming dairy to meet nutritional needs.

Fermented foods were a staple in the Viking diet, offering both preservation and enhanced nutritional value. Honey has integrated fermented foods into his vegetarian diet as well, including items such as sauerkraut, kimchi, and tempeh. These foods not only add unique flavors and textures to his meals but also provide probiotics and enzymes that aid in digestion and support immune function.

Natural Sweeteners and Herbs: Enhancing Flavor and Health

The Viking diet, though simple, was rich in flavor due to the use of natural sweeteners and herbs. Honey was a common sweetener, and herbs like dill, thyme, and juniper added depth to their meals.

In his vegetarian diet, Honey emphasizes the use of natural, unrefined sweeteners and a variety of herbs and spices to enhance both the flavor and nutritional value of his food.

Honey uses natural sweeteners like raw honey, maple syrup, and dates in moderation, recognizing their benefits over refined sugars. These sweeteners provide a natural source of energy and contain trace nutrients that support overall health. By using these sweeteners sparingly, Honey is able to enjoy the sweetness in his meals while maintaining a balanced diet.

Herbs and spices play a significant role in Honey's cooking, much like they did in the Viking diet. He incorporates a wide range of herbs and spices, including turmeric, ginger, garlic, and rosemary, which not only enhance the flavor of his dishes but also offer various health benefits. These herbs are known for their anti-inflammatory, antioxidant, and immune-boosting properties, making them a valuable addition to Honey's diet.

Sustainability and Mindful Eating in a Vegetarian Context

The Vikings lived in harmony with their environment, using resources sustainably and ensuring that nothing went to waste. Honey has adopted a similar approach to his vegetarian diet, prioritizing sustainability and mindful eating practices that support both his health and the health of the planet.

Honey is committed to sourcing his food from local, organic, and sustainable producers. He understands that the choices he makes as a consumer have a direct impact on the environment, and he strives to minimize his ecological footprint by choosing foods that are grown and produced in an environmentally responsible manner. This includes supporting local farmers, reducing food waste, and choosing plant-based foods that require fewer resources to produce than animal-based products.

Mindful eating is another key aspect of Honey's

approach to diet and nutrition. He practices mindfulness at every meal, taking the time to savor each bite, appreciate the flavors and textures of his food, and tune into his body's hunger and fullness cues. This practice not only enhances his enjoyment of food but also helps him make more intentional and health-conscious choices.

By integrating sustainability and mindful eating into his vegetarian diet, Honey is able to create a lifestyle that supports both his well-being and the health of the planet. This approach reflects the Viking values of living in harmony with nature and making choices that honor both the individual and the community.

The Modern-Day Vegetarian Viking Diet

Honey's vegetarian diet, while different from the traditional Viking diet, is deeply rooted in the same principles of simplicity, sustainability, and nourishment. By focusing on whole, natural foods, prioritizing plant-based proteins, and embracing sustainability and mindfulness, Honey has created a diet that supports his health, vitality, and overall well-being.

This modern-day interpretation of the Viking diet demonstrates that the core principles of the Norse approach to eating can be adapted to fit a vegetarian lifestyle, offering a guide to healthy, balanced, and sustainable living. Whether through his emphasis on high-quality plant-based proteins, his focus on whole grains and vegetables, or his commitment to sustainability and mindful eating, Honey's diet reflects a deep understanding of the importance of nutrition in supporting a healthy, balanced, and fulfilling life.

Feasting and Fasting: Balancing Celebration and Discipline

Feasting and fasting were integral practices in Viking culture, reflecting a balance between abundance and restraint. The Vikings celebrated their victories and harvests with grand feasts, yet they also practiced fasting during times of scarcity, which helped them maintain discipline and resilience. Honey Makhija, while following a vegetarian lifestyle, has embraced these principles in his own life, using feasting and fasting as tools to maintain both physical and mental discipline while also enjoying the pleasures of life.

The Role of Feasting in a Vegetarian Lifestyle

Feasting was a significant aspect of Viking culture, serving as a time for celebration, community, and the sharing of abundance. These feasts were not just about the food; they were about the experience of coming together, sharing stories, and strengthening bonds. Honey has adopted this approach to feasting in his vegetarian lifestyle, recognizing the importance of celebration and community in a balanced and fulfilling life.

For Honey, feasting is about more than just indulging in food; it is about creating meaningful experiences and connections with others. Whether it's a holiday celebration, a family gathering, or a special occasion, Honey believes in the importance of coming together to share a meal and to celebrate the moments that make life meaningful. His vegetarian feasts are rich in flavor, creativity, and variety, reflecting his commitment to quality and nourishment.

Honey's feasts often feature a variety of vegetarian dishes that highlight the abundance of plant-based foods. These meals include a wide range of vegetables, grains, legumes, and dairy products, all prepared with care and attention to detail. Honey takes pride in creating dishes that are not only delicious but also visually appealing, making his feasts a celebration of both food and artistry.

While the Vikings may have celebrated with an abundance of meat and ale, Honey's vegetarian feasts focus on plant-based abundance, with dishes that are hearty, satisfying, and full of flavor. Whether it's a rich vegetable stew, a flavorful grain salad, or a decadent dessert made with natural sweeteners, Honey's feasts are a testament to the idea that vegetarian food can be both indulgent and nourishing.

The Discipline of Fasting in a Vegetarian Context

Just as the Vikings practiced fasting during times of scarcity, Honey incorporates intermittent fasting into his vegetarian lifestyle as a way to maintain discipline, support his health, and optimize his energy levels. Intermittent fasting involves alternating periods of eating with periods of fasting, and it has been shown to have a range of health benefits, including improved metabolic function, increased fat loss, and enhanced cognitive function.

Honey typically follows a 16/8 intermittent fasting schedule, which involves fasting for 16 hours and eating during an 8-hour window. During his fasting period, Honey consumes water, herbal teas, and black coffee, which help to keep him hydrated and energized while also supporting the fasting process. This schedule allows him to enjoy the benefits of fasting while still having the flexibility to enjoy meals with family and friends.

For Honey, intermittent fasting is not just about the physical benefits; it is also a way to cultivate mental discipline and to develop a deeper awareness of his body's needs. Fasting requires mindfulness and self-control, qualities that Honey values and seeks to cultivate in all areas of his life. By practicing fasting, Honey is able to maintain a sense of balance and discipline, even as he enjoys the occasional feast and celebration.

Honey's approach to intermittent fasting is characterized by flexibility and balance. He listens to his body and adjusts his fasting schedule as needed, recognizing that flexibility is key to maintaining a sustainable and healthy fasting practice. By incorporating intermittent fasting into his routine, Honey is able to maintain his physical and mental discipline while also enjoying the occasional feast and celebration.

Balancing Celebration and Discipline in a

Vegetarian Diet

For Honey, the key to maintaining a healthy and balanced approach to diet and nutrition is finding the right balance between celebration and discipline. He understands that life is meant to be enjoyed, and that food is one of life's great pleasures. At the same time, he recognizes the importance of maintaining discipline and making choices that support his health and well-being.

Honey's approach to balancing celebration and discipline is rooted in the principles of moderation and mindfulness. He believes that it is possible to enjoy life's pleasures, including good food and drink, without compromising one's health. By practicing moderation and being mindful of his choices, Honey is able to indulge in the occasional feast without feeling guilty or sacrificing his health goals.

This balance between celebration and discipline is also reflected in Honey's approach to social occasions. He understands that food is an important part of social gatherings and that it plays a key role in bringing people together. However, he also knows that it is possible to enjoy these occasions without overindulging. By focusing on quality, choosing nutritious foods, and being mindful of portion sizes, Honey is able to enjoy social occasions while still maintaining his commitment to health and wellness.

The Role of Ritual in Feasting and Fasting

For the Vikings, feasting and fasting were often accompanied by rituals and traditions that added meaning and significance to these practices. Whether it was offering a toast to the gods, sharing stories around the fire, or observing certain customs during times of scarcity, these rituals helped to create a sense of community and connection.

Honey has also incorporated rituals into his approach to feasting and fasting, recognizing the importance of creating meaning and intention around these practices. During feasts and celebrations, Honey often takes the time to express gratitude for the food and the company, recognizing the importance of these moments in his life. He also uses these occasions as an opportunity to connect with loved ones, to share stories, and to create lasting memories.

Similarly, during his fasting periods, Honey practices mindfulness and reflection, using the time to tune into his body's signals and to cultivate a deeper awareness of his physical and mental state. He may use this time for meditation, journaling, or simply being present with his thoughts, recognizing that fasting is not just about abstaining from food, but also about creating space for reflection and self-awareness.

By incorporating rituals into his feasting and fasting practices, Honey is able to add depth and meaning to these experiences, making them more than just about food. These rituals help to create a sense of connection, both to himself and to others, and they serve as a reminder of the importance of balance, moderation, and mindfulness in all aspects of life.

The Benefits of Feasting and Fasting in a Vegetarian Lifestyle

Honey has found that the practice of balancing feasting and fasting offers a range of benefits, both physical and mental. On a physical level, intermittent fasting has helped Honey maintain a healthy weight, improve his metabolic function, and increase his energy levels. It has also helped him develop a deeper awareness of his body's hunger and fullness cues, allowing him to make more mindful and intentional food choices.

On a mental level, fasting has helped Honey cultivate discipline, focus, and resilience. The practice of abstaining from food for a period of time requires mental strength and determination, and Honey has found that this discipline carries over into other areas of his life. Fasting has also provided Honey with an opportunity for reflection and self-awareness, helping him to develop a deeper connection with his body and mind.

Feasting, on the other hand, has provided Honey with a sense of joy, celebration, and connection. By allowing himself to enjoy the occasional feast, Honey is able to experience the pleasure of good food and good company without guilt or regret. These feasts also provide Honey with an opportunity to connect with loved ones, to celebrate life's milestones, and to create meaningful experiences and memories.

Overall, the practice of balancing feasting and fasting has allowed Honey to create a diet and lifestyle that is both enjoyable and sustainable. By embracing both celebration and discipline, Honey is able to maintain his health and well-being while also enjoying the pleasures of life. This balance is a reflection of the Viking approach to diet and nutrition, where both feasting and fasting played an important role in maintaining physical and mental resilience.

Incorporating Feasting and Fasting into a

Vegetarian Lifestyle

For those looking to incorporate the principles of feasting and fasting into their own vegetarian lifestyle, Honey offers several practical tips and insights. First and foremost, Honey emphasizes the importance of listening to one's body and finding a balance that works for each individual. While intermittent fasting has worked well for Honey, he acknowledges that it may not be suitable for everyone, and he encourages others to experiment and find an approach that aligns with their unique needs and goals.

Honey also emphasizes the importance of quality over quantity when it comes to feasting. He encourages others to focus on choosing high-quality, nutritious foods that support health and well-being, even during celebrations. By prioritizing quality, it is possible to enjoy the pleasures of good food without compromising one's health goals.

Finally, Honey encourages the practice of

mindfulness and intentionality when it comes to both feasting and fasting. Whether it's savoring each bite during a feast or tuning into one's body during a fast, mindfulness helps to create a deeper connection with food and to cultivate a more balanced and healthy relationship with eating.

Conclusion

Honey Makhija's approach to diet and nutrition is deeply rooted in the principles of the Viking diet, emphasizing whole, natural foods, sustainability, and a balanced approach to eating. By adopting these principles within a vegetarian framework, Honey has been able to create a diet that supports his physical, mental, and emotional well-being, while also reflecting his commitment to health, discipline, and mindful living.

Through his practice of balancing feasting and fasting, Honey has found a way to enjoy the pleasures of good food and celebration while also maintaining his discipline and focus. This balance is a reflection of the Viking approach to life, where both celebration and discipline played an important role in maintaining resilience and well-being.

Honey's diet and nutrition practices offer valuable lessons for those seeking to lead a healthier, more balanced life. By embracing the principles of whole foods, sustainability, and mindfulness, and by finding a balance between celebration and discipline, it is possible to create a diet and lifestyle that supports both health and happiness in a vegetarian context.

Chapter - 5

Spirituality and Mindfulness

The Vikings were deeply spiritual people, with their beliefs and practices woven into the fabric of their daily lives. Their spirituality was not confined to places of worship but permeated every aspect of existence, influencing their actions, decisions, and interactions with the world around them. Norse mythology, with its rich pantheon of gods, tales of heroism, and belief in fate, served as a guide for the Vikings, helping them navigate the challenges of life with courage and purpose. In the modern world, where spirituality can often be sidelined in the rush of daily life, Honey Makhija has found inspiration in these ancient beliefs, integrating spirituality and mindfulness into his life in ways that guide his actions, focus his mind, and help him live with intention and purpose.

Norse Mythology and Beliefs: Guiding Principles for Modern Life

Norse mythology is rich with stories of gods, giants, and heroes, each embodying different aspects of human experience. These myths were not just stories for the Vikings; they were lessons, allegories, and moral guides that informed their worldview and behavior. The values embodied in these myths—courage, honor, loyalty, and the acceptance of fate—were central to Viking life, helping them face challenges with strength and resolve. Honey Makhija, while not a follower of Norse mythology in a literal sense, has drawn on these ancient stories and the values they represent to shape his own spiritual practices and guiding principles.

The Influence of Norse Mythology

The stories of Norse mythology are filled with powerful themes that resonate deeply with the human experience. The tales of Odin, Thor, Loki, and other gods explore the complexities of life—courage in the face of danger, the struggle between good and evil, the inevitability of fate, and the importance of wisdom and knowledge. These stories were passed down through generations, serving as both entertainment and moral instruction for the Vikings.

Honey has found in these stories a source of inspiration and guidance. While he does not practice Norse mythology as a religion, he has adopted the values and lessons from these myths as part of his spiritual framework. For Honey, these stories are not just ancient tales but timeless lessons that offer insight into how to live a meaningful and purposeful life.

For instance, the story of Odin, the Allfather, who sacrificed one of his eyes to gain wisdom, resonates with Honey's own commitment to lifelong learning and personal growth. Odin's pursuit of knowledge, even at great personal cost, serves as a reminder that wisdom is invaluable and that the quest for understanding is a noble pursuit. Honey has integrated this lesson into his life by prioritizing education, self-reflection, and the continuous expansion of his knowledge base.

Another story that has influenced Honey is the tale of Thor, the god of thunder, known for his strength and bravery. Thor's battles against the forces of chaos and his unwavering commitment to protecting his people are emblematic of the Viking values of courage and loyalty. Honey sees in Thor's story a model for how to face challenges in life—with strength, determination, and a sense of responsibility to those around him. This has translated into Honey's approach to leadership and his dedication to his family and community.

The Concept of Fate in Norse Belief

One of the most compelling aspects of Norse mythology is the belief in fate, or *Wyrd*. The Vikings believed that fate was a powerful and inescapable force, woven by the Norns—mysterious beings who controlled the destinies of gods and men alike.

While the Vikings accepted the inevitability of fate, they also believed in the importance of making choices that aligned with their values and principles, even in the face of inevitable outcomes.

Honey has found a deep connection with this concept of fate, interpreting it not as a predetermined destiny, but as a recognition that while some aspects of life are beyond our control, we have the power to shape our response to them. This understanding has helped Honey cultivate a sense of acceptance and peace with the uncertainties of life, while also empowering him to take deliberate and purposeful action in the areas he can influence.

For Honey, the concept of fate serves as a reminder to focus on what truly matters—living with integrity, making decisions that reflect his values, and maintaining a sense of purpose in all that he does. This approach allows him to navigate the complexities of life with a balanced perspective, acknowledging the forces beyond his control while taking responsibility for his actions and choices.

The Role of Ritual in Spiritual Practice

Rituals played a central role in Viking spirituality, serving as a way to honor the gods, mark important events, and connect with the spiritual realm. These rituals were often simple yet powerful, involving offerings, prayers, and symbolic actions that reinforced the Vikings' connection to their beliefs and the world around them.

Honey has incorporated the concept of ritual into his own spiritual practices, recognizing the importance of creating space for reflection, intention, and connection. While his rituals may not involve the same elements as those of the Vikings, they serve a similar purpose—grounding him in his values and helping him maintain a sense of spiritual alignment in his daily life.

One of Honey's key rituals is a daily practice of setting intentions. Each morning, Honey takes a few moments to reflect on his goals for the day and to align his actions with his broader values and purpose. This practice, inspired by the Viking tradition of preparing for the day's challenges with a clear mind and focused spirit, helps Honey approach his day with clarity and determination.

Another ritual Honey practices is a regular reflection on his personal and professional life. Much like the Vikings would gather around the fire to tell stories and reflect on their experiences, Honey takes time each week to review his progress, celebrate his achievements, and identify areas for growth. This ritual of reflection not only keeps Honey aligned with his goals but also reinforces his commitment to continuous improvement and personal development.

Building a Personal Belief System

While Honey draws inspiration from Norse mythology, his spiritual practices are not confined to any one tradition or belief system. Instead, he has built a personal belief system that integrates elements from various spiritual traditions, philosophies, and teachings that resonate with him.

This eclectic approach allows Honey to create a spiritual framework that is both meaningful and practical, guiding his actions and decisions in a way that aligns with his values.

Honey's belief system is centered around the principles of integrity, responsibility, and purpose. He believes in living a life that reflects these values, making choices that are guided by a sense of moral responsibility and a commitment to contributing positively to the world. This belief system informs every aspect of Honey's life, from his personal relationships to his business decisions, ensuring that he remains true to his core values in all that he does.

One of the key tenets of Honey's belief system is the idea of interconnectedness—the understanding that all aspects of life are interconnected and that our actions have far-reaching effects. This concept, which is echoed in many spiritual traditions, including Norse mythology, has inspired Honey to approach life with a sense of humility and responsibility, recognizing the impact of his choices on others and the world around him.

Honey also incorporates elements of mindfulness and meditation into his belief system, recognizing the importance of staying present and connected to the moment. These practices help Honey maintain a sense of balance and inner peace, allowing him to navigate the challenges of life with a calm and centered mind.

By building a personal belief system that draws on the wisdom of various traditions, Honey has created a spiritual framework that is both flexible and deeply rooted in his values. This system not only guides his actions and decisions but also provides him with a sense of purpose and meaning in his life.

Mindfulness Practices: Staying Focused and Living with Purpose

Mindfulness, the practice of staying present and fully engaged in the moment, has become an essential tool for navigating the complexities of modern life. While the Vikings may not have used the term "mindfulness," their approach to life—marked by focus, intention, and a deep connection to the present—embodies many of the principles that define mindfulness today. Honey Makhija has embraced mindfulness as a central component of his spiritual practice, using it to stay focused, live with purpose, and cultivate a sense of inner peace and clarity.

The Practice of Mindfulness

Mindfulness is the practice of bringing one's full attention to the present moment, without judgment or distraction. It involves being fully aware of one's thoughts, feelings, and sensations, and observing them with curiosity and acceptance. For Honey, mindfulness is not just a practice but a way of life, one that informs how he approaches every aspect of his day.

Honey's mindfulness practice begins each morning with meditation. He sets aside time to sit in stillness, focusing on his breath and grounding himself in the present moment. This practice helps Honey clear his mind of distractions and set a calm and focused tone for the day ahead. By starting his day with mindfulness, Honey is able to approach his tasks with greater clarity and intention, ensuring that he remains aligned with his goals and values.

Throughout the day, Honey incorporates mindfulness into his routine in various ways. Whether it's taking a few deep breaths before starting a new task, practicing mindful eating during meals, or taking a moment to appreciate the beauty of nature during a walk, Honey uses these moments of mindfulness to stay connected to the present and to cultivate a sense of calm and presence.

Mindfulness also plays a key role in how Honey manages stress and challenges. When faced with difficult situations, Honey turns to mindfulness to help him stay grounded and centered. By focusing on his breath and bringing his attention to the present moment, Honey is able to respond to challenges with greater clarity and composure, rather than reacting impulsively or being overwhelmed by stress.

Meditation: A Path to Clarity and Inner Peace

Meditation is a cornerstone of Honey's mindfulness practice, providing him with a dedicated time and space to cultivate inner peace, clarity, and self-awareness. Through meditation, Honey is able to quiet his mind, connect with his inner self, and gain insight into his thoughts and emotions. This practice not only enhances Honey's ability to stay focused and present but also helps him develop a deeper understanding of himself and his place in the world.

Honey practices various forms of meditation, each serving a different purpose. One of his primary practices is breath-focused meditation, where he concentrates on his breath as a way to anchor his mind and bring himself into the present moment. This practice helps Honey calm his mind, reduce stress, and cultivate a sense of inner peace.

In addition to breath-focused meditation, Honey also practices visualization meditation. During these sessions, Honey visualizes his goals, intentions, and desired outcomes, creating a mental image of the life he wants to create. This practice not only helps Honey stay focused on his goals but also reinforces his belief in the power of intention and positive thinking.

Honey also incorporates loving-kindness meditation into his practice, a form of meditation that involves sending goodwill, compassion, and loving energy to oneself and others. This practice helps Honey cultivate a sense of connection and empathy, both for himself and for those around him. By focusing on the well-being of others, Honey is able to strengthen his sense of compassion and contribute positively to the world.

Meditation, for Honey, is more than just a relaxation technique; it is a spiritual practice that deepens his connection to himself and the world around him. Through meditation, Honey is able to access a deeper level of awareness and insight, guiding his actions and decisions in a way that aligns with his values and purpose.

Mindful Reflection: Learning and Growing from Experience

Reflection is a key component of Honey's mindfulness practice, providing him with the opportunity to learn from his experiences and grow as an individual. Much like the Vikings would reflect on their experiences to gain wisdom and insight, Honey uses reflection as a tool for personal and professional development.

Each evening, Honey sets aside time for mindful reflection, reviewing the events of the day and considering what went well, what challenges arose, and what lessons can be learned. This practice allows Honey to gain insight into his actions and decisions, identify areas for improvement, and celebrate his successes. By reflecting on his experiences, Honey is able to continuously learn and grow, both personally and professionally.

Honey also uses reflection as a way to stay connected to his values and purpose. By regularly checking in with himself and evaluating whether his actions align with his goals and values, Honey is able to maintain a sense of integrity and purpose in all that he does. This practice of reflection not only keeps Honey grounded but also helps him stay focused on what truly matters, ensuring that he remains on the path that leads to his desired outcomes.

The Role of Gratitude in Mindfulness

Gratitude is an integral part of Honey's mindfulness practice, helping him cultivate a positive mindset and appreciate the abundance in his life. The Vikings, despite the hardships they faced, were known for their ability to find joy and contentment in the simple things, and Honey has embraced this attitude of gratitude as part of his spiritual practice.

Each day, Honey takes time to reflect on the things he is grateful for, whether it's the support of his loved ones, the opportunities he has been given, or the beauty of the natural world. By focusing on gratitude, Honey is able to shift his perspective from what is lacking to what is present, fostering a sense of contentment and fulfillment.

Gratitude also plays a key role in how Honey approaches challenges. Rather than viewing difficulties as setbacks, Honey sees them as opportunities for growth and learning. By practicing gratitude for the lessons that challenges bring, Honey is able to maintain a positive and resilient mindset, even in the face of adversity.

Honey's practice of gratitude extends beyond his personal life to his interactions with others. He makes it a point to express appreciation for the people in his life, whether it's through a kind word, a thoughtful gesture, or simply taking the time to acknowledge their contributions. This practice not only strengthens Honey's relationships but also reinforces his commitment to living with compassion and empathy.

Mindfulness in Action: Applying Principles to Daily Life

For Honey, mindfulness is not just a practice to be done in quiet moments; it is a way of being that permeates every aspect of his life. He strives to apply the principles of mindfulness—presence, intention, and non-judgment—to his daily actions, decisions, and interactions.

In his professional life, Honey uses mindfulness to stay focused and present during meetings, negotiations, and decision-making processes. By bringing his full attention to each task, Honey is able to approach his work with clarity and precision, ensuring that he makes informed and thoughtful decisions. This mindful approach to business not only enhances Honey's effectiveness as a leader but also fosters a positive and productive work environment.

In his personal life, Honey applies mindfulness to his relationships, ensuring that he is fully present and engaged with the people who matter most to him. Whether it's spending quality time with family, listening attentively to a friend, or simply being present in the moment with a loved one, Honey uses mindfulness to strengthen his connections and cultivate meaningful relationships.

Honey also applies mindfulness to his self-care practices, recognizing the importance of taking care of his physical, mental, and emotional well-being. By practicing mindful eating, exercise, and relaxation, Honey ensures that he is nourishing his body and mind in a way that supports his overall health and vitality.

The Benefits of Mindfulness and Spirituality

Honey has found that integrating mindfulness and spirituality into his life offers a range of benefits, both tangible and intangible. On a physical level, mindfulness practices such as meditation and mindful eating have helped Honey reduce stress, improve focus, and enhance his overall well-being. These practices have also contributed to Honey's ability to maintain a healthy work-life balance, ensuring that he remains energized and resilient in the face of life's challenges.

On a mental and emotional level, mindfulness and spirituality have provided Honey with a sense of clarity, purpose, and inner peace. By staying connected to his values and maintaining a sense of presence in the moment, Honey is able to navigate life's complexities with greater ease and confidence. These practices have also helped Honey cultivate a positive and compassionate mindset, allowing him to approach challenges with resilience and grace.

Spiritually, Honey's practices have deepened his connection to himself and the world around him, providing him with a sense of meaning and fulfillment. By drawing on the wisdom of Norse mythology and other spiritual traditions, Honey has created a belief system that guides his actions and decisions, helping him live a life that is aligned with his values and purpose.

Conclusion

Honey Makhija's approach to spirituality and mindfulness is deeply inspired by the values and practices of the Vikings, adapted to fit the context of modern life. By drawing on the wisdom of Norse mythology, building a personal belief system, and integrating mindfulness into his daily routine, Honey has created a spiritual framework that guides his actions, informs his decisions, and helps him live with intention and purpose.

Through practices such as meditation, mindful reflection, and gratitude, Honey is able to stay focused, maintain inner peace, and cultivate a positive and resilient mindset. These practices not only enhance Honey's personal and professional life but also provide him with a sense of connection, meaning, and fulfillment.

Honey's spiritual and mindfulness practices offer valuable lessons for those seeking to live a more intentional and purposeful life. By embracing the principles of presence, intention, and non-judgment, and by staying connected to one's values and purpose, it is possible to navigate life's challenges with clarity, resilience, and grace. Honey's approach serves as a powerful reminder of the importance of spirituality and mindfulness in creating a life that is not only successful but also deeply meaningful and fulfilling.

Chapter - 6

Community and Kinship

The Vikings were a people deeply rooted in community and kinship, understanding that their strength and survival depended on the bonds they forged with those around them. In a harsh and often unforgiving world, the Vikings relied on their communities for support, protection, and a sense of belonging. These bonds were not just based on family ties but extended to the broader community, including friends, neighbors, and allies. The Vikings celebrated these connections through feasts, rituals, and shared endeavors, all of which reinforced their sense of unity and purpose.

In modern times, the importance of community and kinship remains as vital as ever. Honey Makhija has embraced these principles in his own life, dedicating himself to building a strong and supportive community around him. Through his businesses, philanthropic efforts, and personal relationships, Honey fosters a sense of belonging and unity, much like the Vikings who understood that their true strength lay in their connections with others.

Build a Strong Community: Honey's Dedication to Support and Unity

Building a strong community is a cornerstone of Honey Makhija's life philosophy. He understands that individual success is deeply intertwined with the well-being of the community and that true fulfillment comes from contributing to something larger than oneself. For Honey, community is not just about proximity or social interaction; it is about creating a network of support, trust, and shared values that enriches the lives of everyone involved.

The Importance of Community in Business

Honey's commitment to community begins with his approach to business. He believes that a successful business is one that not only generates profit but also contributes positively to the community it serves. This belief is reflected in the way Honey conducts his business, ensuring that his companies are not just commercial enterprises but also vehicles for social good.

One of the ways Honey builds community through his businesses is by fostering a workplace culture that values collaboration, respect, and mutual support. He understands that employees are the backbone of any organization, and he is dedicated to creating an environment where they feel valued, empowered, and connected. Honey's businesses prioritize open communication, transparency, and inclusivity, ensuring that every team member feels like they are part of a larger mission.

Honey also emphasizes the importance of giving

back to the community through his businesses. He believes that companies have a responsibility to contribute to the social and economic well-being of the communities in which they operate. To this end, Honey's businesses engage in various initiatives that support local development, education, and environmental sustainability. These efforts not only benefit the community but also strengthen the bonds between the business and the people it serves.

One notable example of Honey's commitment to community is his involvement in local education initiatives. Recognizing the importance of education in breaking the cycle of poverty and fostering social mobility, Honey has partnered with schools and educational institutions to provide scholarships, mentorship programs, and resources for students from underprivileged backgrounds. By investing in education, Honey is not only contributing to the development of future generations but also helping to build a more equitable and thriving community.

Philanthropy as a Means of Building Community

Philanthropy is another key aspect of Honey's approach to building community. He believes that those who have the means to do so have a responsibility to give back and support those in need. Honey's philanthropic efforts are driven by a deep sense of empathy and a desire to make a meaningful impact on the lives of others.

Honey's philanthropic initiatives are diverse, ranging from supporting healthcare and education to promoting environmental sustainability and social justice. What sets Honey's approach to philanthropy apart is his focus on building long-term, sustainable solutions rather than simply providing short-term aid. He understands that true community-building requires addressing the root causes of social issues and empowering individuals and communities to take control of their own futures.

One of Honey's flagship philanthropic initiatives is the establishment of the Honey Makhija Foundation, which focuses on providing access to basic necessities such as food, clean water, and healthcare to underserved communities. The foundation operates on the principle of "community empowerment," working closely with local leaders and organizations to ensure that the initiatives are tailored to the specific needs of each community. By involving the community in the decision-making process, Honey ensures that the solutions are not only effective but also sustainable in the long term.

Honey also recognizes the importance of economic empowerment in building strong communities. Through his foundation, he has launched several programs aimed at providing vocational training, entrepreneurship support, and microfinance opportunities to individuals in marginalized communities. These programs help individuals gain the skills and resources they need to start their own businesses, create jobs, and contribute to the economic development of their communities.

Mentorship and Leadership Development

Another way Honey builds community is through mentorship and leadership development. He believes that strong communities are built on strong leaders, and he is committed to nurturing the next generation of leaders who will continue to drive positive change in their communities.

Honey takes an active role in mentoring young entrepreneurs, professionals, and community leaders, providing them with the guidance, support, and resources they need to succeed. He understands that leadership is not just about achieving personal success but about empowering others and creating opportunities for collective growth. Through one-on-one mentorship, workshops, and leadership development programs, Honey helps emerging leaders develop the skills, confidence, and vision they need to make a difference in their communities.

Honey's mentorship approach is rooted in the values of empathy, integrity, and collaboration. He encourages his mentees to lead with compassion, to prioritize ethical decision-making, and to build inclusive teams that reflect the diversity of the communities they serve. By instilling these values in the next generation of leaders, Honey is helping to create a ripple effect that will strengthen communities for years to come.

Creating a Sense of Belonging

At the heart of Honey's community-building efforts is the belief that everyone deserves to feel a sense of belonging. He understands that a strong community is one where individuals feel connected, valued, and supported, and he works tirelessly to create spaces where people can come together, share experiences, and build lasting relationships.

One of the ways Honey fosters a sense of belonging is through the creation of community spaces that bring people together. Whether it's through the design of his business offices, the establishment of community centers, or the organization of public events, Honey prioritizes the creation of environments that encourage social interaction and connection. These spaces are designed to be inclusive and welcoming, reflecting Honey's commitment to creating communities where everyone feels they belong.

Honey also recognizes the importance of cultural and social events in fostering a sense of community. He regularly organizes and supports events that celebrate the diversity, history, and traditions of the communities he is a part of. These events provide opportunities for people to come together, share their stories, and celebrate their commonalities and differences. By creating spaces for cultural exchange and social interaction, Honey helps to build stronger, more connected communities.

Collaborative Community Projects

Collaboration is a key element of Honey's community-building strategy. He believes that the most effective solutions are those that are developed in partnership with the community and that draw on the collective strengths and resources of all stakeholders. Honey's approach to community projects is based on collaboration, bringing together businesses, nonprofits, government agencies, and community members to work toward common goals.

One example of Honey's collaborative approach to community-building is his involvement in a large-scale urban renewal project. Recognizing the need for affordable housing and community development in a disadvantaged neighborhood, Honey brought together a diverse group of stakeholders, including local government officials, real estate developers, community leaders, and residents, to create a comprehensive plan for revitalizing the area.

The project focused not only on building

affordable housing but also on creating green spaces, improving infrastructure, and providing access to essential services such as healthcare, education, and transportation. By working collaboratively, the project was able to address the multiple needs of the community and create a sustainable, long-term solution that benefited everyone involved.

Honey's collaborative approach extends beyond physical infrastructure to include social programs that address the needs of vulnerable populations. Through partnerships with local organizations, Honey has helped to launch programs that provide support for at-risk youth, seniors, and individuals experiencing homelessness. These programs offer a range of services, including job training, mental health support, and housing assistance, all aimed at helping individuals regain their independence and become active participants in their communities.

By focusing on collaboration and inclusivity, Honey has been able to create community projects that not only address immediate needs but also lay the groundwork for long-term social and economic development. His approach reflects the Viking tradition of working together to achieve common goals, recognizing that true strength lies in unity and cooperation.

Celebrate Together: Fostering a Sense of Belonging and Unity

The Vikings were known for their feasts and celebrations, which served as important social events that reinforced community bonds and celebrated shared values. These gatherings were more than just opportunities to eat and drink; they were occasions to honor the gods, commemorate victories, and strengthen the ties between family, friends, and allies. Honey Makhija has embraced this tradition of celebration, using gatherings with family, friends, and colleagues as a way to foster a sense of belonging, unity, and shared purpose.

The Importance of Celebration in Building Community

Honey believes that celebration plays a crucial role in building and maintaining strong communities. He understands that coming together to celebrate achievements, milestones, and special occasions not only strengthens relationships but also creates a sense of shared identity and purpose. For Honey, these gatherings are opportunities to connect with others, express gratitude, and reinforce the values that bind the community together.

One of the ways Honey fosters a sense of belonging through celebration is by hosting regular gatherings for his family, friends, and colleagues. These events are carefully planned to ensure that everyone feels included and valued, with a focus on creating an atmosphere of warmth, hospitality, and togetherness. Whether it's a formal dinner, a casual barbecue, or a festive holiday party, Honey's gatherings are designed to bring people together and create lasting memories.

Honey also recognizes the importance of

acknowledging and celebrating the achievements of individuals within the community. He makes it a point to celebrate the successes of his team members, whether it's a promotion, a completed project, or a personal milestone. By taking the time to recognize and celebrate these achievements, Honey reinforces the idea that everyone's contributions are valued and that the success of the community is built on the success of its members.

Family Gatherings: Strengthening Kinship Bonds

For the Vikings, kinship bonds were the foundation of their social structure, and family gatherings were essential for maintaining these connections. Honey has carried this tradition into his own life, placing a high value on family gatherings as a way to strengthen kinship bonds and create a sense of unity and belonging.

Honey's family gatherings are regular occurrences, bringing together multiple generations to share meals, stories, and experiences. These gatherings are more than just social events; they are opportunities for the family to reconnect, reflect on their shared history, and reinforce their commitment to one another. Honey believes that these gatherings are essential for maintaining the strength and resilience of the family unit, particularly in a fast-paced and often fragmented modern world.

During these family gatherings, Honey makes it a point to create an environment where everyone feels welcome and included. He encourages open communication, active listening, and mutual respect, ensuring that every family member has a voice and feels valued. By fostering a sense of belonging and inclusion, Honey helps to build a strong and supportive family community that can weather any challenge.

Honey also places a strong emphasis on tradition during family gatherings. He believes that traditions provide a sense of continuity and connection, linking the past with the present and future. Whether it's a traditional holiday meal, a special family recipe, or a cultural celebration, Honey incorporates these traditions into his gatherings, helping to preserve the family's heritage and create a sense of shared identity.

Celebrating with Friends and Colleagues

In addition to family gatherings, Honey also places a high value on celebrating with friends and colleagues. He understands that strong social bonds are essential for personal and professional well-being, and he makes it a priority to create opportunities for these bonds to flourish.

Honey regularly hosts social events for his friends and colleagues, ranging from informal get-togethers to more structured events such as team-building retreats and professional development workshops. These gatherings provide an opportunity for individuals to connect on a personal level, share ideas, and build relationships outside of the formal work environment.

One of the key elements of Honey's approach to

celebrating with friends and colleagues is his focus on creating a positive and inclusive atmosphere. He believes that these gatherings should be spaces where everyone feels comfortable, appreciated, and able to express themselves freely. To this end, Honey ensures that his events are inclusive of diverse perspectives, cultures, and experiences, reflecting his commitment to building a community that values and celebrates diversity.

Honey also uses these gatherings as an opportunity to recognize and celebrate the collective achievements of his team. Whether it's a successful project, a new business milestone, or a community initiative, Honey takes the time to acknowledge the hard work and dedication of his colleagues. By celebrating these successes together, Honey reinforces the idea that the achievements of the individual contribute to the success of the whole community.

Cultural and Social Celebrations

Cultural and social celebrations play an

important role in fostering a sense of community and belonging, and Honey is a strong advocate for these types of events. He believes that celebrating cultural diversity and social achievements helps to build bridges between different groups, promote understanding, and strengthen the bonds within the community.

Honey is actively involved in organizing and supporting cultural events that celebrate the heritage and traditions of the communities he is part of. Whether it's a festival, a cultural exhibition, or a community fair, Honey sees these events as opportunities to bring people together, share cultural experiences, and promote a sense of unity and pride.

One example of Honey's commitment to cultural celebration is his involvement in organizing an annual multicultural festival in his community. The festival showcases the diverse cultures represented in the area, featuring music, dance, food, and art from different cultural groups. The event not only celebrates the richness of cultural diversity but also provides a platform for cross-cultural exchange and dialogue.

Honey also supports social celebrations that honor the achievements and contributions of community members. These events, such as award ceremonies, community recognition dinners, and volunteer appreciation events, highlight the positive impact that individuals have on their communities and reinforce the values of service, leadership, and collaboration.

By supporting and participating in cultural and social celebrations, Honey helps to create a sense of pride, unity, and shared purpose within the community. These events serve as reminders that, despite our differences, we are all part of the same community and that our collective strength lies in our ability to come together and celebrate what makes us unique.

The Power of Shared Experiences

At the heart of Honey's approach to community

and kinship is the belief in the power of shared experiences. He understands that it is through these shared experiences—whether it's a family gathering, a community celebration, or a collaborative project—that bonds are formed, trust is built, and a sense of belonging is created.

Honey believes that these shared experiences are essential for building a strong and resilient community. They provide opportunities for individuals to connect on a deeper level, to share their stories, and to support one another. These experiences also create a sense of continuity and connection, linking the past with the present and future.

Honey's commitment to creating and supporting shared experiences is evident in everything he does, from his personal relationships to his professional endeavors. He sees these experiences as the building blocks of community and kinship, and he is dedicated to fostering an environment where they can flourish.

Conclusion

Honey Makhija's approach to community and kinship is deeply rooted in the values and traditions of the Vikings, adapted to fit the context of modern life. Through his dedication to building a strong and supportive community, fostering a sense of belonging and unity, and celebrating the achievements and diversity of those around him, Honey has created a network of connections that enriches the lives of everyone involved.

Honey's commitment to community is reflected in his approach to business, philanthropy, mentorship, and celebration. Whether it's through creating inclusive work environments, supporting local development initiatives, mentoring the next generation of leaders, or hosting gatherings that bring people together, Honey is dedicated to building a community that is strong, resilient, and united by shared values and purpose.

Through his efforts, Honey has demonstrated that true strength lies in the connections we build with others and that by coming together to celebrate, support, and uplift one another, we can create communities that are not only successful but also deeply fulfilling and meaningful. Honey's approach serves as a powerful reminder of the importance of community and kinship in creating a life that is rich in connection, purpose, and joy.

Chapter - 7

Explore and Adventure

The Vikings were renowned for their spirit of exploration and adventure, venturing into unknown territories with courage and curiosity. They sailed across vast oceans, discovered new lands, and traded with distant civilizations, leaving a lasting legacy of bravery and discovery. This spirit of exploration was not limited to physical voyages but also extended to the pursuit of knowledge and new skills, as they constantly sought to expand their understanding and capabilities.

In modern times, the spirit of exploration and adventure remains a powerful force that drives individuals to push boundaries, embrace new experiences, and pursue personal and professional growth. Honey Makhija embodies this Viking spirit through his ventures into new markets, personal travel experiences, and relentless pursuit of knowledge and skills. His journey is marked by a deep curiosity, an openness to new experiences, and a commitment to continuous learning and development.

Travel and Explore: Embodying the Viking Spirit of Exploration

From a young age, Honey has been fascinated by the world beyond his immediate surroundings. This curiosity has led him on numerous journeys across the globe, both in his professional endeavors and personal life. Through his travels, Honey has gained invaluable experiences, broadened his perspectives, and forged meaningful connections that have enriched his life and work.

Venturing into New Markets: Navigating Uncharted Territories

In the world of business, exploration often means venturing into new markets and industries, seeking opportunities for growth and innovation. Honey has consistently demonstrated a bold and adventurous approach to business, embracing challenges and risks with the same fervor and determination that characterized the Viking explorers.

Identifying Opportunities in Emerging Markets

Honey's journey into new markets began early in his career when he recognized the immense potential of emerging economies. While many of his contemporaries focused on established markets, Honey saw opportunities in regions that were often overlooked or considered too risky. He understood that with careful research, strategic planning, and a willingness to adapt, these markets could offer significant rewards.

One of Honey's notable ventures was his entry into the Southeast Asian market. Recognizing the region's rapid economic growth, youthful population, and increasing connectivity, Honey saw an opportunity to expand his business operations and tap into a burgeoning consumer base. He conducted extensive market research, analyzing economic indicators, consumer behavior, and local business practices to develop a comprehensive understanding of the landscape.

Building Local Partnerships and Understanding Cultural Nuances

Understanding that successful expansion requires more than just identifying opportunities, Honey focused on building strong local partnerships and immersing himself in the cultural nuances of the region. He engaged with local business leaders, government officials, and community members to gain insights and establish trust. Honey believed that respecting and understanding local cultures was essential for sustainable and ethical business practices.

In Indonesia, for example, Honey partnered with a local entrepreneur to launch a technology startup focused on providing digital solutions for small and medium-sized enterprises (SMEs). This partnership combined Honey's expertise in technology and business development with the local partner's deep understanding of the market and cultural context. Together, they navigated regulatory challenges, adapted their business model to local needs, and built a successful enterprise that empowered local businesses and contributed to economic growth.

Adapting to Challenges and Learning from Failures

Venturing into new markets is fraught with challenges and uncertainties, and Honey's experiences were no exception. He encountered numerous obstacles, including complex regulatory environments, fierce competition, and unforeseen economic shifts. However, Honey viewed these challenges as opportunities for learning and growth.

In one instance, Honey attempted to enter the African market with a renewable energy project aimed at providing sustainable energy solutions to rural communities.

Despite thorough planning and significant investment, the project faced numerous setbacks, including logistical difficulties and regulatory hurdles. Instead of viewing the venture as a failure, Honey analyzed the experience to identify what went wrong and how he could improve in future endeavors. He recognized the need for deeper engagement with local stakeholders, more flexible business models, and greater resilience in the face of adversity.

This reflective approach allowed Honey to refine his strategies and successfully launch subsequent projects in other regions. He embraced the lessons learned from setbacks, much like the Vikings who adapted their strategies based on their experiences, learning from each voyage and continuously improving their navigation and seafaring skills.

Innovating and Disrupting Established

Industries

Honey's spirit of exploration also extends to his willingness to challenge and disrupt established industries. He is constantly seeking innovative solutions and new ways of doing things, pushing the boundaries of what is possible.

In the finance sector, Honey launched a fintech startup that aimed to democratize access to financial services through innovative technology solutions. Recognizing that traditional banking systems often excluded large segments of the population, particularly in developing countries, Honey sought to create a platform that provided accessible, affordable, and user-friendly financial services.

The venture involved extensive research and development, collaboration with technology experts, and navigating complex regulatory frameworks. Honey's team developed cutting-edge technologies, such as blockchain and artificial intelligence, to create secure and efficient financial products. The startup faced skepticism and resistance from established financial institutions, but Honey's persistence and innovative approach eventually led to widespread adoption and significant impact on financial inclusion.

Personal Travel Experiences: Expanding Horizons and Cultivating Empathy

Beyond his professional endeavors, Honey's personal travels have played a significant role in shaping his worldview and personal development. He views travel not just as a leisure activity but as a profound learning experience that offers insights into different cultures, histories, and ways of life.

Immersive Cultural Experiences

Honey approaches travel with an open mind and a desire to immerse himself fully in the cultures he encounters. He seeks out authentic experiences, engages with local communities, and embraces the unfamiliar with enthusiasm and respect.

During a journey through Scandinavia, Honey sought to connect with the roots of Viking culture that have long inspired him. He visited historical sites, such as the Viking Ship Museum in Oslo and the ancient trading town of Birka in Sweden. Honey participated in local traditions, tasted traditional foods, and even joined a reenactment of a Viking voyage, sailing on a replica longship across the Norwegian fjords.

These immersive experiences deepened Honey's appreciation for the resilience, ingenuity, and adventurous spirit of the Vikings. He drew parallels between their explorations and his own journeys, finding inspiration in their courage and adaptability.

Developing Global Perspectives and Cultural Sensitivity

Traveling extensively has allowed Honey to develop a broad and nuanced understanding of the world. He has visited countries across Asia, Africa, Europe, and the Americas, each journey offering new insights and perspectives.

In India, Honey spent time volunteering with a

local nonprofit organization focused on education and community development. He lived with a host family, learned about the challenges and aspirations of the community, and contributed his skills and resources to support local initiatives. This experience fostered a deep sense of empathy and reinforced Honey's commitment to social responsibility and community engagement.

In Japan, Honey explored the intersection of tradition and modernity, marveling at how ancient customs coexist with cutting-edge technology. He studied the principles of Kaizen (continuous improvement) and Zen philosophy, integrating these concepts into his personal and professional life. These experiences enriched Honey's leadership style, emphasizing mindfulness, efficiency, and a balanced approach to progress.

Adventure and Personal Growth

For Honey, travel is also about embracing adventure and pushing personal boundaries. He seeks out experiences that challenge him physically, mentally, and emotionally, fostering resilience and self-discovery.

On a trek through the Himalayas, Honey faced harsh weather conditions, physical exhaustion, and the mental challenges of navigating rugged terrain. The journey tested his endurance and resolve, but also offered moments of profound beauty and reflection. Reaching the summit, Honey felt a deep sense of accomplishment and a renewed appreciation for nature's grandeur and his own capabilities.

Similarly, Honey embarked on a solo journey through the Amazon rainforest, immersing himself in one of the world's most diverse and complex ecosystems. He learned survival skills, connected with indigenous communities, and gained a deeper understanding of environmental conservation and sustainability.

These adventures have not only provided Honey with thrilling experiences but have also contributed significantly to his personal growth. They have taught him valuable lessons in resilience, adaptability, and self-reliance, qualities that he carries into all aspects of his life.

Connecting and Networking Across Cultures

Honey also leverages his travels to build a diverse and expansive network of connections across the globe. He understands the importance of relationships and collaborations in today's interconnected world and seeks to forge meaningful connections wherever he goes.

Through attending international conferences, participating in cultural exchanges, and engaging in global forums, Honey has built relationships with individuals from various backgrounds and industries. These connections have opened doors to new opportunities, facilitated cross-cultural collaborations, and enriched Honey's understanding of global trends and dynamics.

In Africa, Honey connected with social entrepreneurs working on innovative solutions to local challenges. Collaborations emerged, leading to joint ventures and shared initiatives that combined resources and expertise to create meaningful impact.

These global networks also serve as a source of inspiration and learning for Honey. Engaging with diverse perspectives and experiences challenges his assumptions, stimulates creative thinking, and keeps him attuned to emerging ideas and innovations.

Learn New Skills: Reflecting the Viking's Thirst for New Challenges

The Vikings were not only explorers but also skilled craftsmen, traders, and warriors. They valued learning and mastery, constantly honing their skills and acquiring new knowledge to adapt to changing environments and seize new opportunities. Honey mirrors this relentless pursuit of knowledge and skills, dedicating himself to continuous learning and personal development across various domains.

Embracing Lifelong Learning

Honey firmly believes that learning is a lifelong journey and that personal and professional growth requires constant acquisition and refinement of skills. He approaches learning with enthusiasm and curiosity, seeking out new challenges and opportunities to expand his knowledge base.

Pursuing Academic and Professional Education

Honey's commitment to learning is evident in his academic and professional pursuits. He holds multiple degrees and certifications across diverse fields, reflecting his wide-ranging interests and dedication to excellence.

After completing his undergraduate studies in business administration, Honey pursued a master's degree in international relations to deepen his understanding of global dynamics and geopolitics. Recognizing the growing importance of technology in business, he later enrolled in a specialized program in information technology management, equipping himself with the skills to navigate and leverage digital transformations.

Honey also participates in executive education programs and professional workshops, staying updated on the latest trends and best practices in leadership, innovation, and management. He values formal education as a foundation for structured learning and professional credibility, but also recognizes the importance of practical experience and informal learning.

Developing New Skills in Business and Entrepreneurship

As an entrepreneur, Honey is constantly seeking to develop new skills that enhance his effectiveness and adaptability in a rapidly changing business landscape.

Mastering Strategic Thinking and Decision-Making

Honey has dedicated significant time to mastering strategic thinking and decision-making skills. He studies various strategic frameworks and methodologies, applies them in real-world scenarios, and reflects on the outcomes to refine his approach.

He engages with mentors and thought leaders, participates in strategy workshops, and studies case studies of successful and failed businesses to understand the nuances of effective decision-making. Honey also practices scenario planning and risk assessment, developing the ability to anticipate and navigate complex and uncertain environments.

Enhancing Communication and Negotiation Skills

Recognizing the critical role of communication in leadership and business success, Honey has invested in developing strong communication and negotiation skills. He attends public speaking courses, practices active listening, and seeks feedback to improve his clarity, persuasion, and empathy in communication.

Honey also studies negotiation techniques,

learning to navigate complex negotiations with confidence and skill. He applies these skills in various contexts, from business deals to conflict resolution, achieving outcomes that are mutually beneficial and sustainable.

Learning About Emerging Technologies

In an era of rapid technological advancement, Honey prioritizes learning about emerging technologies and understanding their implications for business and society. He takes courses in areas such as artificial intelligence, blockchain, and data analytics, attends technology conferences, and collaborates with tech experts to stay at the forefront of innovation. This knowledge enables Honey to identify and leverage technological opportunities, drive digital transformation in his businesses, and make informed decisions about technology investments and strategies.

Exploring Creative and Artistic Pursuits

Honey's thirst for knowledge and new skills extends beyond the business realm into creative and artistic pursuits. He believes that engaging in creative activities enhances cognitive abilities, fosters innovation, and enriches personal fulfillment.

Writing and Storytelling

One of Honey's passions is writing and storytelling. He sees storytelling as a powerful tool for communication, connection, and inspiration. Honey has taken writing courses, participated in writers' workshops, and dedicates time to crafting stories that convey meaningful messages and reflect his experiences and insights.

He has written articles and essays on topics ranging from leadership and entrepreneurship to travel and personal development, sharing his knowledge and perspectives with a broader audience. Honey is also working on a memoir that chronicles his journey and the lessons he has learned along the way, aiming to inspire others to pursue their dreams and embrace life's adventures.

Learning Music and Musical Instruments

Honey has also pursued musical education, learning to play instruments such as the guitar and piano. He views music as a universal language that transcends cultural and linguistic barriers, offering a profound means of expression and connection.

Learning music has taught Honey discipline, patience, and the joy of creative expression. He enjoys performing for friends and family, using music as a way to bring people together and create shared experiences.

Engaging in Visual Arts

Exploring visual arts, Honey has taken up photography and painting, mediums that allow him to capture and interpret the world around him in unique and creative ways. Through photography, he documents his travels and experiences, capturing moments of beauty, emotion, and significance. Painting offers Honey a different form of expression, enabling him to explore colors, forms, and textures to convey moods and ideas.

These creative pursuits not only provide Honey

with personal fulfillment and relaxation but also enhance his observational skills, creativity, and appreciation for diverse forms of expression.

Cultivating Physical and Mental Skills

Honey understands the importance of balancing mental and physical development and engages in activities that challenge and strengthen both aspects.

Learning Martial Arts

Inspired by the Viking warrior ethos, Honey has pursued training in various martial arts, including Muay Thai and Brazilian Jiu-Jitsu. These disciplines have taught him self-defense skills, physical fitness, and mental discipline. Through rigorous training and practice, Honey has developed resilience, focus, and confidence that translate into other areas of his life.

Practicing Mindfulness and Meditation

To cultivate mental clarity and emotional balance, Honey practices mindfulness and meditation. He has studied various meditation techniques, attended retreats, and integrated mindfulness practices into his daily routine. These practices help Honey manage stress, enhance focus, and maintain a grounded and balanced approach to life and work.

Learning Languages

Honey's global travels and business ventures have motivated him to learn multiple languages, including Spanish, Mandarin, and French. Language learning enables him to communicate more effectively, understand different cultures deeply, and build stronger connections across diverse communities.

He approaches language learning through formal courses, immersive experiences, and consistent practice, appreciating the cognitive benefits and cultural insights that come with mastering new languages.

Embracing New Challenges and Stepping Out of Comfort Zones

Central to Honey's pursuit of new skills is his

willingness to embrace challenges and step out of his comfort zone. He understands that true growth occurs when one confronts uncertainty and pushes beyond perceived limitations.

Public Speaking and Leadership Roles

Despite initially feeling nervous about public speaking, Honey challenged himself by taking on speaking engagements and leadership roles that required him to address large audiences. Through practice, feedback, and perseverance, he transformed a personal challenge into a strength, becoming a confident and inspiring speaker who effectively communicates his vision and ideas.

Engaging in Challenging Projects and Initiatives

Honey deliberately takes on projects and initiatives that stretch his capabilities and expose him to new experiences. Whether it's leading a complex business merger, organizing a large-scale community event, or participating in endurance sports competitions, Honey seeks out opportunities that challenge him to learn, adapt, and grow.

Learning from Mentors and Role Models

Throughout his journey, Honey has sought guidance and inspiration from mentors and role models across various fields. He values the wisdom and experience that others can offer and actively seeks opportunities to learn from their insights and examples.

He connects with leaders, experts, and thinkers through networking, mentorship programs, and collaborative projects, engaging in meaningful dialogues and exchanges that enhance his understanding and capabilities. Honey also studies the lives and works of historical figures and contemporary influencers, drawing lessons and inspiration from their achievements and challenges.

Sharing Knowledge and Teaching Others

Honey believes that learning is a reciprocal process and that teaching others is a powerful way to reinforce and expand one's own knowledge. He actively shares his skills and experiences through mentoring, teaching workshops, and contributing to educational initiatives.

By helping others learn and grow, Honey not only contributes to the development of his community but also deepens his understanding and mastery of the subjects he teaches. This commitment to sharing knowledge reflects the Viking tradition of passing down skills and wisdom through generations, ensuring the continued growth and prosperity of the community.

Conclusion

Honey Makhija's journey of exploration and adventure is a testament to his embodiment of the Viking spirit in the modern world. Through his ventures into new markets, immersive travel experiences, and relentless pursuit of knowledge and skills, Honey demonstrates courage, curiosity, and a commitment to continuous growth and discovery.

His willingness to embrace uncertainty, adapt to new environments, and learn from diverse experiences has enabled Honey to achieve remarkable success and personal fulfillment. He approaches life as an ongoing adventure, filled with opportunities to explore, learn, and connect.

Honey's example serves as an inspiration for others to cultivate their own spirit of exploration and learning. By stepping beyond comfort zones, seeking new experiences, and dedicating oneself to lifelong learning, individuals can expand their horizons, unlock their potential, and lead rich and meaningful lives.

In a world that is constantly evolving and presenting new challenges, the spirit of exploration and the thirst for knowledge remain vital forces that drive innovation, resilience, and progress. Honey's journey reminds us that by embracing adventure and committing to learning, we can navigate the complexities of our world with confidence, adaptability, and purpose, creating fulfilling lives and contributing positively to the world around us.

Chapter - 8

Warrior Mindset

The Viking warriors were legendary for their mental toughness, resilience, and unwavering determination in the face of adversity. Their lives were filled with challenges, from navigating treacherous seas to engaging in fierce battles, yet they approached these obstacles with a fearless mindset and a commitment to overcoming any hurdle. This warrior mentality, deeply ingrained in Viking culture, was not just about physical strength but also about mental fortitude, strategic thinking, and an unyielding belief in one's ability to prevail.

In the modern world, the concept of a warrior mindset transcends the battlefield, applying to all areas of life where challenges and adversities arise. Honey Makhija exemplifies this mindset in his approach to business, personal growth, and daily life. Through his mental toughness, resilience, and preparedness, Honey navigates the complexities of life with the same courage and determination that defined the Viking warriors. Whether through literal practices of self-defense or metaphorical strategies in business, Honey's warrior mindset enables him to face challenges head-on and emerge stronger.

Mental Toughness: Building Resilience in the Face of Adversity

Mental toughness is the cornerstone of a warrior mindset. It is the ability to remain focused, determined, and composed in the face of challenges, setbacks, and uncertainty. For Honey, mental toughness is not just an innate trait but a skill that can be cultivated and strengthened over time. Through deliberate practice, reflection, and a commitment to growth, Honey has developed a robust mental resilience that allows him to push through adversity and thrive in difficult circumstances.

Embracing Challenges as Opportunities for

Growth

Honey's journey has been marked by numerous challenges, both personal and professional. Rather than shying away from these difficulties, Honey views them as opportunities for growth and self-improvement. He believes that challenges are an inevitable part of life and that how one responds to them is what truly defines success.

One of the key elements of Honey's mental toughness is his ability to reframe challenges as learning experiences. When faced with a setback, Honey doesn't dwell on the negative aspects but instead focuses on what can be learned from the situation. This mindset allows him to extract valuable lessons from every experience, using them to inform future decisions and strategies.

For example, early in his career, Honey faced a significant financial loss due to a failed business venture. While many might have been discouraged or even devastated by such a setback, Honey chose to view it as a critical learning experience. He conducted a thorough analysis of what went wrong, identifying areas where he could improve his decision-making and risk management. This reflective approach not only helped Honey recover from the loss but also equipped him with the insights needed to succeed in subsequent ventures.

Developing a Growth Mindset

Central to Honey's mental toughness is his commitment to a growth mindset—the belief that abilities and intelligence can be developed through dedication and hard work. This mindset is the foundation of Honey's approach to life, driving him to continuously seek out new challenges and opportunities for personal development.

Honey's growth mindset is evident in his willingness to step outside his comfort zone and embrace new experiences, even when they are daunting or unfamiliar. Whether it's learning a new skill, entering a new market, or taking on a leadership role, Honey approaches each challenge with the belief that he can grow and improve through effort and perseverance.

This mindset also helps Honey maintain a positive attitude in the face of setbacks. Instead of seeing failure as a reflection of his abilities, Honey views it as a natural part of the learning process. This perspective allows him to remain resilient and motivated, even when things don't go as planned.

Building Emotional Resilience

Emotional resilience is a critical component of mental toughness, enabling individuals to cope with stress, maintain emotional balance, and recover quickly from setbacks. Honey has developed strong emotional resilience through practices that help him manage stress and maintain a positive outlook.

One of Honey's key practices for building emotional resilience is mindfulness meditation. By regularly engaging in mindfulness, Honey cultivates a sense of inner calm and clarity that allows him to navigate stressful situations with composure. This practice helps him stay present, avoid being overwhelmed by negative emotions, and maintain focus on his goals.

Honey also practices gratitude as a way to strengthen his emotional resilience. By focusing on the positive aspects of his life, even during difficult times, Honey is able to maintain a sense of perspective and prevent stress from taking over. This practice of gratitude helps him stay grounded and reminds him of the bigger picture, which is essential for maintaining mental toughness.

Facing Adversity with Courage and Determination

Courage is a defining characteristic of the Viking warrior mindset, and it is also a key aspect of Honey's approach to life. Honey believes that courage is not the absence of fear but the willingness to face fear and adversity with determination and resolve.

Throughout his life, Honey has faced numerous situations that required him to summon his courage and take decisive action. Whether it was making difficult business decisions, standing up for his values, or navigating personal challenges, Honey has consistently demonstrated the ability to act with courage, even when the stakes were high.

One notable example of Honey's courage in the face of adversity was his decision to leave a secure and high-paying job to pursue his entrepreneurial dreams. This decision required him to step into the unknown, leaving behind the stability of a corporate career to embrace the risks and uncertainties of entrepreneurship. Despite the fear and doubt that accompanied this decision, Honey remained steadfast in his commitment to his vision, trusting in his ability to navigate the challenges that lay ahead.

This courage has also been evident in Honey's response to personal challenges. For instance, when faced with a serious health scare, Honey approached the situation with the same resilience and determination that he brings to his professional life. He sought out the best medical care, educated himself about his condition, and took proactive steps to manage his health. Throughout the process, Honey remained focused on his recovery and committed to maintaining a positive attitude, even in the face of uncertainty.

Strategic Thinking and Problem-Solving

Mental toughness is not just about emotional resilience; it also involves the ability to think strategically and solve problems effectively. Honey has honed his strategic thinking skills through years of experience, study, and reflection, enabling him to approach challenges with a clear and analytical mindset.

When faced with a complex problem, Honey takes a methodical approach, breaking the issue down into manageable parts and considering various solutions. He draws on his knowledge, experience, and intuition to evaluate the potential outcomes of different strategies, ensuring that his decisions are well-informed and aligned with his goals.

Honey also values the importance of seeking diverse perspectives when solving problems. He often consults with mentors, colleagues, and experts in different fields to gain insights and feedback. This collaborative approach not only enhances the quality of his decision-making but also helps Honey build a network of support that he can rely on in times of need.

Honey's ability to think strategically and solve problems under pressure has been a key factor in his success. Whether navigating a business crisis, managing a team conflict, or addressing a personal challenge, Honey's mental toughness and problem-solving skills enable him to find effective solutions and move forward with confidence.

Self-Defense: Preparedness in Business and Life

The concept of self-defense extends beyond physical combat; it encompasses the idea of being prepared, both mentally and strategically, to protect oneself and one's interests in various aspects of life. For Honey, self-defense is not just about physical training but also about being equipped with the knowledge, skills, and mindset needed to navigate challenges and protect his well-being.

Physical Self-Defense and Martial Arts

Honey has a strong interest in physical fitness and self-defense, recognizing the importance of being physically prepared to protect oneself and others. He has trained in various martial arts, including Muay Thai and Brazilian Jiu-Jitsu, disciplines that require not only physical strength and agility but also mental focus and discipline.

The Benefits of Martial Arts Training

Martial arts training has provided Honey with a range of physical and mental benefits. Physically, it has helped him build strength, endurance, and flexibility, all of which contribute to overall health and well-being. The rigorous training routines and techniques have also improved Honey's coordination, reflexes, and balance, making him more agile and capable in various physical activities.

Mentally, martial arts have taught Honey the importance of discipline, focus, and perseverance. The practice requires a high level of concentration and mental clarity, as well as the ability to remain calm and composed in high-pressure situations. These mental attributes are not only valuable in self-defense scenarios but also translate into other areas of life, including business and personal relationships.

The Philosophy of Martial Arts

Beyond the physical techniques, martial arts have instilled in Honey a philosophy of respect, humility, and self-control. He has learned that true strength lies not in aggression but in the ability to manage one's emotions and respond to situations with wisdom and restraint. This philosophy is reflected in Honey's approach to conflict resolution, where he prioritizes finding peaceful and constructive solutions rather than resorting to confrontation.

Honey's martial arts training also emphasizes the importance of continuous learning and self-improvement. Just as in other areas of his life, Honey approaches martial arts with a growth mindset, constantly seeking to refine his skills and deepen his understanding of the discipline. This commitment to mastery and personal development is a key aspect of Honey's warrior mindset.

Preparedness in Business: Strategic Self-Defense

In the business world, self-defense takes on a different meaning, encompassing the strategies and practices that protect a company's interests, reputation, and long-term viability. Honey applies the principles of self-defense to his business endeavors, ensuring that he is well-prepared to navigate challenges, mitigate risks, and safeguard his company's success.

Risk Management and Contingency Planning

One of the key aspects of business self-defense is

risk management. Honey recognizes that every business venture carries inherent risks, and he takes a proactive approach to identifying and mitigating these risks. He conducts thorough risk assessments for each project, considering potential challenges and developing contingency plans to address them. Honey's risk management strategy involves diversifying investments, maintaining financial reserves, and building strong relationships with key stakeholders. By being prepared for potential setbacks, Honey ensures that his businesses can withstand unforeseen challenges and continue to thrive.

Protecting Intellectual Property and Competitive Advantage

In today's competitive business environment, protecting intellectual property and maintaining a competitive advantage are critical aspects of self-defense. Honey is vigilant about safeguarding his company's intellectual assets, including trademarks, patents, and proprietary information.

He works closely with legal experts to ensure that all necessary protections are in place and that his company's innovations and brands are secure.

Honey also emphasizes the importance of continuous innovation as a form of self-defense. By staying ahead of industry trends, investing in research and development, and fostering a culture of creativity, Honey ensures that his businesses remain competitive and adaptable to changing market conditions.

Crisis Management and Reputation Protection

Another critical aspect of business self-defense is crisis management. Honey understands that in the age of social media and instant communication, a company's reputation can be impacted by crises or negative events. To protect against this, Honey has developed comprehensive crisis management plans that outline how to respond to various scenarios, from product recalls to public relations challenges. Honey's crisis management strategy includes clear communication protocols, designated response teams, and regular training for employees. By being prepared for potential crises, Honey ensures that his businesses can respond swiftly and effectively, minimizing damage and protecting their reputation.

Emotional Self-Defense: Protecting Mental and Emotional Well-Being

Self-defense is not limited to physical and business strategies; it also involves protecting one's mental and emotional well-being. Honey recognizes that maintaining mental and emotional resilience is essential for long-term success and fulfillment, and he has developed practices that help him manage stress, maintain balance, and protect his mental health.

Setting Boundaries and Prioritizing Self-Care

One of Honey's key strategies for emotional self-defense is setting clear boundaries and prioritizing self-care. He understands that in order to be effective in his work and personal life, he must first take care of himself. This involves setting limits on his work hours, delegating tasks when necessary, and making time for rest, relaxation, and activities that bring him joy.

Honey also practices self-compassion, recognizing that it's okay to take breaks and that self-care is not a luxury but a necessity. By prioritizing his well-being, Honey ensures that he has the energy, focus, and resilience needed to face challenges and achieve his goals.

Managing Stress Through Mindfulness and Relaxation Techniques

Stress is an inevitable part of life, especially for someone as driven and ambitious as Honey. However, he has developed effective strategies for managing stress and protecting his mental health. One of these strategies is the regular practice of mindfulness meditation, which helps Honey stay grounded, centered, and present in the moment.

Honey also incorporates relaxation techniques such as deep breathing exercises, progressive muscle relaxation, and visualization into his daily routine. These practices help him release tension, reduce anxiety, and maintain a calm and focused mindset, even in the midst of stressful situations.

Building a Support Network

Another important aspect of emotional self-defense is building a strong support network. Honey surrounds himself with positive, supportive people who uplift and encourage him. He values the importance of close relationships with family, friends, and mentors, and he regularly seeks out their guidance, feedback, and companionship.

Honey also recognizes the importance of seeking professional support when needed. He is not afraid to reach out to therapists, coaches, or counselors when facing significant challenges or emotional difficulties. By building and maintaining a robust support network, Honey ensures that he has the resources and support needed to navigate life's challenges with resilience and strength.

Facing Life's Battles with a Warrior's Spirit

Whether in business, personal growth, or daily life, Honey approaches challenges with the mindset of a warrior. He understands that life is filled with battles—some big, some small—and that the key to overcoming them is not just physical or strategic strength, but mental and emotional resilience.

Honey's warrior mindset is characterized by his commitment to continuous learning, his willingness to face adversity with courage and determination, and his ability to adapt and persevere in the face of setbacks. He embodies the Viking spirit of resilience, preparedness, and unwavering resolve, using these qualities to achieve success and fulfillment in all areas of his life.

Conclusion

Honey Makhija's warrior mindset is a testament to his resilience, mental toughness, and preparedness in the face of life's challenges. Through his dedication to personal growth, strategic thinking, and self-defense—both literal and metaphorical—Honey navigates the complexities of life with the same courage and determination that defined the Viking warriors.

His ability to embrace challenges as opportunities for growth, develop emotional resilience, and protect his mental and physical well-being reflects a deep commitment to living with purpose and intention. Honey's warrior mindset not only enables him to achieve his goals but also inspires others to cultivate their own resilience, adaptability, and strength.

In a world where challenges are inevitable and change is constant, the warrior mindset serves as a powerful tool for navigating adversity, achieving success, and living a fulfilling life. Honey's journey reminds us that true strength lies not just in physical power but in the ability to face life's battles with courage, resilience, and an unwavering belief in our own potential. By cultivating a warrior mindset, we can all become better equipped to handle the challenges of life and emerge stronger, wiser, and more empowered.

Conclusion: Living the Modern Viking Life

The Vikings were more than just seafaring warriors; they were explorers, craftsmen, traders, and community builders whose values and principles have endured through the ages. Their resilience, courage, and commitment to community and kinship allowed them to thrive in some of the harshest environments known to humanity. The Viking spirit, characterized by a blend of toughness, curiosity, and a deep connection to nature and community, continues to inspire people today.

In a world that is increasingly complex and fast-paced, the principles of Viking life offer timeless wisdom that can guide us toward a more balanced, purposeful, and fulfilling existence. By embodying these values in his life, Honey Makhija serves as a modern-day exemplar of the Viking spirit. His journey provides a roadmap for how we can apply these ancient principles to our own lives, blending the wisdom of the past with the demands of modern living.

Living the Modern Viking Life: Applying Viking Principles in the Contemporary World

The idea of living a modern Viking life is not about emulating the exact lifestyle of the Norsemen, but rather about embracing the core values that defined their culture. These values—courage, resilience, community, exploration, and a deep connection to nature—are as relevant today as they were over a thousand years ago. The key is to adapt these principles to our current circumstances, using them as a guide to navigate the complexities of contemporary life.

Embracing Courage and Resilience

At the heart of the Viking ethos is the concept of courage—facing challenges head-on, even when the odds are against you. In today's world, courage is about stepping out of your comfort zone, taking calculated risks, and pursuing your passions despite the uncertainties that lie ahead. It's about having the mental toughness to persevere in the face of adversity, much like the Vikings who sailed into the unknown with little more than their instincts and the strength of their community.

Honey Makhija exemplifies this courage in his approach to business, personal growth, and life's challenges. Whether it's venturing into new markets, overcoming setbacks, or pursuing his entrepreneurial dreams, Honey demonstrates that courage is not the absence of fear, but the willingness to move forward despite it. By adopting a courageous mindset, we can push our limits, discover new possibilities, and achieve our goals.

Resilience is another fundamental Viking trait that is essential for modern living. The ability to bounce back from setbacks, adapt to changing circumstances, and continue striving toward your goals is critical in a world that is constantly evolving. Honey's life is a testament to the power of resilience, showing that setbacks are not failures but opportunities to learn, grow, and emerge stronger. To cultivate resilience, it's important to develop a growth mindset, as Honey has done. This involves viewing challenges as learning opportunities, embracing change, and staying focused on long-term goals even when the path is difficult. By building resilience, we can navigate the ups and downs of life with greater ease and maintain our momentum toward success.

Building Strong Communities and Kinship

The Vikings understood that strength lies in community and kinship. Their tight-knit communities provided the support, protection, and resources needed to survive and thrive in a challenging environment. In the modern world, where individualism often takes precedence, the importance of community cannot be overstated. Building and nurturing strong relationships with family, friends, colleagues, and neighbors is essential for creating a sense of belonging, support, and shared purpose. Honey's dedication to building strong communities—whether through his businesses, philanthropic efforts, or personal relationships—highlights the importance of connection in our lives. By fostering a sense of belonging, celebrating achievements together, and supporting one another through challenges, we can create communities that are resilient, thriving, and united by common values.

In practical terms, building a strong community involves investing time and energy in relationships, being present for others, and contributing to the collective well-being. This could mean supporting local initiatives, volunteering, or simply making time for regular gatherings with loved ones. By prioritizing community, we not only enrich our own lives but also contribute to the strength and vitality of those around us.

Exploring and Embracing Adventure

The Vikings were explorers at heart, constantly seeking new lands, opportunities, and experiences. This spirit of exploration is just as important today, whether it's in the context of personal development, career growth, or simply expanding our horizons through travel and learning.

Honey's life is a testament to the value of exploration and adventure. His willingness to venture into new markets, learn new skills, and embrace diverse experiences has not only fueled his personal growth but also driven his success in business. By adopting a similar approach, we can open ourselves up to new possibilities, gain valuable insights, and lead richer, more fulfilling lives. Embracing adventure doesn't necessarily mean traveling to distant lands; it can also involve exploring new ideas, taking on challenging projects, or pursuing hobbies and interests that push us out of our comfort zones. The key is to maintain a sense of curiosity and a willingness to try new things. By doing so, we can continue to grow, learn, and evolve, much like the Vikings who constantly sought to expand their knowledge and capabilities.

Prioritizing Physical Strength and Mental Toughness

Physical strength and mental toughness were essential for the Vikings, enabling them to survive and thrive in a harsh environment. In the modern world, these qualities remain important for maintaining health, well-being, and the ability to face life's challenges with confidence.

Honey's commitment to physical fitness, whether through strength training, martial arts, or other forms of exercise, reflects the Viking emphasis on maintaining a strong and resilient body. Regular physical activity not only improves physical health but also enhances mental clarity, reduces stress, and boosts confidence. By prioritizing physical fitness, we can build the strength and endurance needed to tackle life's challenges head-on.

Mental toughness, as Honey demonstrates, is equally important. Developing resilience, emotional balance, and the ability to stay focused under pressure are critical skills for navigating the complexities of modern life. Practices such as mindfulness, meditation, and stress management techniques can help cultivate mental toughness, allowing us to remain calm, composed, and effective in the face of adversity.

Cultivating a Connection with Nature

The Vikings had a deep connection to the natural world, drawing strength, inspiration, and sustenance from their surroundings. In today's urbanized and technology-driven society, it's easy to become disconnected from nature, but reconnecting with the natural world can have profound benefits for our health, well-being, and sense of purpose.

Honey's efforts to balance his business life with time spent in nature, whether through hiking, retreats, or simply spending time outdoors, highlight the importance of maintaining this connection. Nature offers a space for reflection, relaxation, and rejuvenation, helping us to reset and gain perspective on our lives.

Incorporating nature into our daily routines can be as simple as taking regular walks in the park, practicing outdoor meditation, or spending weekends exploring natural landscapes. By making time for nature, we can reduce stress, enhance our creativity, and foster a deeper sense of connection to the world around us.

Continuing to Learn and Evolve

The Vikings were lifelong learners, constantly honing their skills, acquiring new knowledge, and adapting to changing circumstances. This commitment to continuous learning is a key principle that can guide us in our personal and professional lives.

Honey's pursuit of knowledge, whether through formal education, self-directed learning, or experiential growth, exemplifies the value of continuous development. In a rapidly changing world, the ability to learn, adapt, and evolve is essential for staying relevant, achieving success, and leading a fulfilling life.

We can cultivate this commitment to learning by seeking out new experiences, engaging in lifelong education, and staying curious about the world around us. Whether it's learning a new language, developing a new skill, or exploring a new field of interest, continuous learning keeps our minds sharp, our perspectives broad, and our lives enriched.

Final Thoughts: Balancing Ancient Wisdom with Modern Living

The principles that guided the Viking way of life—courage, resilience, community, exploration, strength, and a deep connection to nature—are timeless and universal. They offer a framework for living a balanced, purposeful, and fulfilling life, even in the midst of the complexities and challenges of the modern world.

Honey Makhija's life serves as a powerful example of how these ancient principles can be applied to contemporary living. Through his dedication to personal growth, his commitment to community, and his willingness to embrace new challenges, Honey embodies the Viking spirit in a way that is both inspiring and practical.

The balance of ancient wisdom with modern living is not about rejecting modernity or romanticizing the past. Instead, it's about integrating the values and practices that have stood the test of time into our current context. By doing so, we can create a life that is not only successful in the conventional sense but also deeply meaningful, connected, and aligned with our true purpose.

The Benefits of Adopting a Viking-Inspired Lifestyle

Adopting a Viking-inspired lifestyle offers numerous benefits for both individuals and communities. By embracing these principles, we can:

1. **Build Resilience and Mental Toughness**: Developing the mental and emotional strength to face challenges with courage and determination allows us to navigate life's ups and downs with confidence and grace.

2. **Foster Strong Relationships and Communities**: Prioritizing connection, kinship, and community-building creates a supportive network that enhances our well-being and contributes to collective success.

3. **Cultivate a Sense of Adventure and Curiosity**: Embracing exploration and continuous learning keeps our minds sharp, our perspectives broad, and our lives enriched with new experiences and knowledge.

4. **Enhance Physical and Mental Well-Being**: Prioritizing physical fitness, mindfulness, and a connection to nature supports overall health, reduces stress, and fosters a sense of balance and fulfillment.

5. **Live with Purpose and Intention**: By aligning our actions with core values such as courage, resilience, and community, we can lead lives that are not only successful but also deeply meaningful and aligned with our

true purpose.

Integrating Viking Principles into Daily Life

The key to integrating Viking principles into daily life is to start small and build gradually. Here are some practical steps to get started:

- **Set Courageous Goals**: Identify areas in your life where you can step out of your comfort zone and take on new challenges. Whether it's pursuing a new career, learning a new skill, or embarking on a personal project, set goals that require courage and determination.

- **Build Resilience**: Practice techniques that strengthen your mental and emotional resilience, such as mindfulness, meditation, and positive self-talk. When faced with setbacks, focus on the lessons learned and use them to inform your future actions.

- **Nurture Your Community**: Invest time in building and maintaining relationships with family, friends, colleagues, and neighbors.

Participate in community activities, offer support to those in need, and celebrate achievements together.

- **Embrace Exploration**: Make time for new experiences, whether it's traveling to a new place, trying a new hobby, or learning something new. Approach life with curiosity and a willingness to explore the unknown.

- **Prioritize Physical Health**: Incorporate regular exercise into your routine, whether it's through strength training, martial arts, or outdoor activities. Focus on building strength, endurance, and flexibility to support overall well-being.

- **Connect with Nature**: Spend time outdoors, whether it's through hiking, gardening, or simply enjoying a walk in the park. Use nature as a space for reflection, relaxation, and rejuvenation.

- **Commit to Lifelong Learning**: Make continuous learning a priority, whether through formal education, online courses, or self-directed study. Stay curious and open to new ideas, and seek out opportunities to expand your knowledge and skills.

A Life of Balance and Fulfillment

In conclusion, the Viking principles of courage, resilience, community, exploration, strength, and a connection to nature offer a powerful framework for living a balanced and fulfilling life. By integrating these principles into our daily lives, we can navigate the complexities of the modern world with confidence, purpose, and a deep sense of fulfillment.

Honey Makhija's journey serves as an inspiring example of how these ancient values can be applied to contemporary living, demonstrating that the wisdom of the past can guide us toward a brighter and more meaningful future. By adopting a Viking-inspired lifestyle, we can build resilience, foster strong communities, embrace new challenges, and live with intention and purpose, creating a life that is not only successful but also deeply enriched by the values that have stood the test of time.

9 789348 037701